The Canadian Short Story

Copyright © 1971 by Holt, Rinehart and Winston of Canada, Limited

All Rights Reserved   ISBN   0-03-923380-4

Cover Design: Bob Frank

Illustrations: Mike Yazzolino

It is illegal to reproduce any portion of this book except by special arrangement with the publishers. Reproduction of this material without authorization by any duplication process whatsoever is a violation of copyright.

Printed in Canada

1 2 3 4 5   75 74 73 72 71

The Canadian Short Story

Tony Kilgallin
University of British Columbia

Holt, Rinehart and Winston of Canada, Limited
Toronto　　　　　　　　　　　　　　　Montreal

General Editor:
Roy Bentley
University of British Columbia
Former co-ordinator of English
Etobicoke Board of Education,
Metropolitan Toronto

Other Titles in the Series

Five Modern Canadian Poets — Eli Mandel
York University

Rhymes and Reasons — John Robert Colombo
Managing Editor
Tamarack Review

Contemporary Satire — David J. Dooley
St. Michael's College
University of Toronto

New Direction in Canadian Poetry — John Robert Colombo
Managing Editor
Tamarack Review

Art, Communication and Pop Kulch — Donald F. Theall
Chairman, Department of English
McGill University

The Screen As Environment — Mark Slade
Director of
Media Study and Research
National Film Board of Canada

The Writing and Reading of Poetry — Earle Birney
Former professor at
University of British Columbia
and award-winning poet

ACKNOWLEDGEMENTS

JONATHAN CAPE LTD.: For "Strange Comfort Afforded by the Profession" from *Hear Us O Lord from Heaven Thy Dwelling Place* by Malcolm Lowry. Reprinted by permission of the Executors of the Malcolm Lowry Estate and Jonathan Cape Ltd.

J. B. LIPPINCOTT COMPANY: For "Strange Comfort Afforded by the Profession" by Malcolm Lowry. Copyright, 1953, by Malcolm Lowry. From the book **Hear Us O Lord From Heaven Thy Dwelling Place** by Malcolm Lowry. Copyright, ©, 1961 by Margerie Bonner Lowry. Reprinted by permission of J. B. Lippincott Company.

McCLELLAND AND STEWART LIMITED, Toronto: For "Some Grist for Mervyn's Mill" from **The Street** by Mordecai Richler.
For "A Kite is a Victim" from **The Spice Box of Earth** by Leonard Cohen.
For "Recipe for a Canadian Novel" from **Abracadabra** by John Robert Colombo. Reprinted by permission of The Canadian Publishers.

JOHN METCALF: For his story "The Happiest Days".

OBERON PRESS: For "Something for Olivia's Scrapbook, I Guess" from **The Streets of Summer** by David Helwig. Used by permission of Oberon Press.

THE RYERSON PRESS: For "Flying A Red Kite" from **Flying A Red Kite** by Hugh Hood.

THE VIKING PRESS, INC.: For "A Kite is a Victim" from **Selected Poems: 1956-1968** by Leonard Cohen. Copyright in all countries of the International Copyright Union. All rights reserved. Reprinted by permission of The Viking Press, Inc.

Care has been exercised to trace ownership of copyright material contained in this text. The publishers will gladly receive information that will enable them to rectify any reference or credit in subsequent editions.

For Eric Satie, Richard Harris, and Chatoyance.

Contents

Introduction   1
    Canadian?   1
    Short Story?   3
        Past and Present   4
        Future   8
    The Creative Process   9
    The Five Fingers of This Anthology   12
    Tradition and Innovation   13

Hugh Hood   19
    Flying A Red Kite   22

David Helwig   33
    Something For Olivia's Scrapbook I Guess   35

John Metcalf   51
    The Happiest Days   53

Mordecai Richler   57
    Some Grist For Mervyn's Mill   59

Malcolm Lowry   83
    Strange Comfort Afforded by the Profession   85

Further Reading for Enjoyment   100

Sources for Reference   103

Introduction

"It is not what a man says, but the part of it which his auditor considers important, that measures the quantity of his communication."

Frobenius

Canadian?

To understand the paradox of this book's title it is necessary to comprehend the artificial standards of nationality by which we prejudge literature. In *Back to Methuselah* Shaw wrote, "what a ridiculous thing to call people Irish because they live in Ireland! You might as well call them Airish because they live in air. They must be just the same as other people." Unfortunately, we cling to the concepts of "Divide and Conquer" and "To Each His Zone". As biased visionaries splitting the single global prism into regionalism, nationalism and internationalism, we risk the *dis-ease* of provincialism. All literatures are initially regional or local, originating in particular places in space and time; how well they travel depends only on the quality of each one's insightful handling of humanity as expressed in the universal matrix of language. Thus, to Pierre Boulez, "Nationalism in music is a disease, a limitation, an excuse for the inexportable." Hemingway agrees:

> No writer worth a damn is a national writer or writer of the frontier or a writer of the Renaissance or a Brazilian writer. Any writer worth a damn is just a writer. That is the hard league to

play in. The ball is standard, the ball parks vary somewhat, but they are all good. There are no bad bounces. Alibis don't count. Go out and do your stuff. You can't do it? Then don't take refuge in the fact that you are a local boy or a rummy, or pant to crawl back into somebody's womb, or have the con or the old râle. You can do it or you can't do it in that league I am speaking of.

If a work is good its creator does not need the crutch of a passport or zip code. Northrop Frye and Marshall McLuhan, are two such global citizens who have understood Canada's true regional identity by temporarily isolating it against a world perspective:

> Canadian literature . . . seems constantly to be trying to understand something that eludes it, frustrated by a sense that there is something to be found that has not been found, something to be heard that the world is too noisy to let us hear. One of the derivations proposed for the word Canada is a Portuguese phrase meaning "nobody here". The etymology of the word Utopia is very similar, and perhaps the real Canada is an ideal with nobody in it. The Canada to which we really do owe loyalty is the Canada we have failed to create. . . . I should like to suggest that our identity, like the real identity of of all nations, is the one that we have failed to achieve. (Frye)

> You can be a French Canadian or an English Canadian but not a Canadian. We know how to live without an identity, and this is one of our marvellous resources. The unity of man is truth. . . . Private identity becomes a meaningless burden in a world when you are totally involved with everyone else. This has happened in the U.S.A. It has not happened in Canada because we have no goals, no commitments. Here is Utopia. We never had the bloodbath necessary to cement a national image. This is a tremendous advantage in the new global theatre—we can play any role we choose. We're not hung-up. So far we've had the advantage of dabbling in identities of being an actor in British, American and French identities. Now we can dabble even further afield. (McLuhan)

So much then for the "Canadian" tag which in literary supermarkets is only a label, not a cherishable product in itself. As a forgotten Canadian once phrased it, "There will never be a Canadian literature until Canadians abandon the delusion that there ever can be such a thing as 'Canadian' literature."

Short Story?

Fragmentation into compartments exists in literature as well as in geography. "Short story", however, defies hard and fast "genre-lie-zings". Generous enough to accommodate a variety of compositions under its namesake, it can loosely be tagged as prose narrative of limited length. In one sense it is the lowest and simplest of literary organisms; in another the highest and most intricate of forms. Dave Godfrey, author of an anthology of stories entitled *Death Goes Better With Coca-Cola*, has commented on the medium as follows:

> The short story is dead, but what form with more potential exists? The novel and poetry are marked, year by year, with battles between new school and newer school, with changing styles and the influence theory and of foreign advances, with high sales and critical acclaim. Terrible distractions. Working in the short narrative form I can project, write, and publish a series of ten to fifteen narratives almost entirely on my own. Fertility is all.

To exemplify its "lowest common denominator" simplicity as well as its complex allegorical suggestion, here is an oral Indian story called "The White Man and the Indian" as translated by Marius Barbeau:

> In the beginning, the white man came to our island. He spoke to our ancestor, who was sitting on the end of a log, "Sit over!" said the white man. The old man moved a little, and allowed the stranger to sit on the log. The newcomer pushed him and repeated, "Sit over!" The Indian moved over a little. But it was

not all. "Move over, I tell you!" And this happened over and over again, until the ancient one found himself at the far end of the log. The white man declared, "Now all the log is mine!"

Pre-literate, tribal and anonymous, such stories together with similar Eskimo legends are the earliest examples in the "Canadian" tradition. Today, post-literate, tribal TV is the latest medium to massage the short story's content. A 1970 adaptation of Morley Callaghan's 1934 tale "Father and Son" changed New York to Toronto, rural Pennsylvania to farmland Ontario, springtime to mid-winter and an arrogant social revolutionary into a contented hippie, yet all without losing the essential "themeanings" of the story. Such improvisation though rare in Indian tales is indicative of the optional variables open to the interplay of modern intermedia.

Past and Present

J. R. Colombo's 1964 poem "Recipe for a Canadian Novel" includes most examples of the Canadian short story before Leacock and Callaghan:

after Cyprian Norwid

Ingredients: one Mountie,
one Indian, an Eskimo
and a Doukhobor.

Add: a small-town whore,
a thousand miles of wheat,
a farmer, impotent and bent.

A fair-haired daughter too,
a Laurentian mountain
and a Montreal Jew.

Include also: a boy
with a dying pet,
and a mortgage unmet

If this sours, sweeten
with maple syrup—
preferably French-Canadian,

but dilute, if foreign
to the taste.
Stir, then beat.

Drop in exotic and tangy
place-names—Toronto,
Saskatoon, Hudson Bay.

To prepare the sauce:
paragraphs of bad prose
that never seem to stop.

For distinctive flavor:
garnish with maple leaves.
Mix, then leave.

Dice one Confederation poet
complete with verse
(remove mold first).

Drain, bring to a simmer,
but avoid a boil.
Pour, place in oven, bake.

Slice in pieces, or leave whole.
Serves nineteen million
when cold.

Strangely enough, stories of the late nineteenth century by Gilbert Parker, Charles G. D. Roberts and Ernest Thompson Seton (see bibliography) sold better in the U.S.A. and England than at home. Parker, born in Ontario, started writing of the Far North which he had never visited, while working as an Australian newspaper editor. His melodramatic hero, Pretty Pierre, galloped through thirty-nine tales of which twenty-seven editions were published in twenty years. Succeeded by Robert Service, Parker appealed to a public greedy for romance and escape fiction; today, the descendants of that public have consumed between 1962 and 1969 over 600 short stories from the hand of Canada's most prolific pop-writer Dan Ross, whose many pseudonyms are found in 22 countries in 13 languages. Still, only 1% of his sales are in Canada.

Leacock's *Sunshine Sketches of a Little Town* (1912) established him as Canada's equivalent to Mark Twain, whom he greatly admired. Perceptive enough to see Canada as an endless series of Mariposas, Leacock anticipated Sinclair Lewis' novel of the same vein *Main Street* (1920), in depicting the triple sunshines of humour, irony and sentiment. Greg Clark, Richard Needham, Eric Nicol and Max Ferguson are four of Leacock's disciples in handling the anecdotal short story with kidding gloves.

The next Canadian writer to innovate the short story was Morley Callaghan, whom Lewis chose over Hemingway in 1929 as his stylistic successor: "Callaghan seems to me particularly to have a really authentic power to making his impressions of life—mad life or lugubriously sane life—completely vivid." In 1950 Malcolm Lowry paid a different tribute to Callaghan's artistry beginning with an exemplary story: "It is informed by a sense of charity and moral meaning that infiltrates down into the story and has the effect of turning much of what normally is known as the organic into something almost superfluous to its intention, while it still remains a work of art." Lowry saw that this quality of parable contained a depth clearly visible on the surface of his stripped, clean, and deceptively easy prose. When asked about his style Callaghan simply repeats, "All I have is my own view of things, through my own eyes and ears. If I try to view things any other way than my own, then it ceases to be me." Combined with the craft of suggesting the implicit in the explicit, the inferred within the stated, is the resonant mystery that exists symbolically perpendicular to the surface of language. The styles of many Canadian writers, including Hood and Metcalf, owe much to his forerunning style.

Hugh Garner shares Callaghan's preoccupation with humanity in the modern cityscape and the latter's concern for morality within reality. Obsessed with a brutal honesty of vision, Garner usually focusses upon society's losers, outsiders and failures, the edge-people whose lives of quiet desperation juggle the occasional gut-responsive bang with the daily whimper. One of Canada's few writers to exist solely upon a literary output, he is pessimistic about the short story's future market. Today, "the untrained short story writer is the result of a lack of suitable markets and his own disinclination to go through a long and heartbreaking apprenticeship in his craft." Unlike Godfrey whose academic post can support his literary projects, Garner is dependent primarily upon the CBC's dramatizations of his works; yet his optimum goal of two good stories a year is insufficient to earn even a subsistence income. To this issue Hugh Hood, another academic, philosophically points out that "cash-nexus economics are the accident of history, stories the permanent possession of mankind."

Robert Weaver of the CBC, broadcaster and editor, has done more for the modern Canadian short story than anyone else. Writers tend to be understandably neurotic, he feels, and need much more than poets a touch of lunacy to keep them at their craft. Call it lunacy or larceny, Margaret Laurence and Mordecai Richler have found that income from other media can enable them to upkeep the costly writing of short stories. Laurence's *A Jest of God*, the model for the movie *Rachel Rachel*, is a creation in the middle range between short story and novel. Richler's movie scriptwriting buys him the time necessary for fiction. It is a great advance from the days when a sale of 50,000 paperbacks earned Hugh MacLennan a gross of only $250, not even enough to pay two months' rent. Still, Metcalf received originally only $25 for the first placement of "The Happiest Days".

Of the 2,500 manuscripts Weaver receives annually, two thirds are good enough to require his final editorial judgment. Slowly disappearing are those submitted by "the little lady writers in tennis shoes. That's the good effect of Canada's being such a discouraging place for writers." The good female writers who remain, Ethel Wilson, Margaret Laurence, Mavis Gallant, Alice Munro, Audrey Thomas, are usually better at experimentation with sensibility than with sensation. Granted that every good story is a blend of both elements, any stress on intuitively felt knowledge, whether psychological or "psocoldlogical" is often handled better by the female who, for the most part, has abandoned the sentimental romanticism that characterized the styles of Lucy Maud Montgomery, Marjorie Pickthall and Mazo de la Roche. Marie-Claire Blais, Marian Engel and Diane Giguere (see bibliography) in particular have attained fine performances to anticipate promising futures. Their styles are the registers of their sensibilities, while their techniques are the externalizations of ideas. As in the works of their male counterparts technique becomes discovery for writer and reader together.

Future

Who needs the short story today? What does it offer that involved journalism, the newspapers, movies and TV cannot? If "the aim of fiction is absolute and honest truth" as Chekhov believed, then the short story can offer the key to liberation from the cell of self. Hugh Hood who on one level holds that "human beings *need* stories just as they need food or sexual activity or religious practice" asserts that "the story-teller's function is that of giving assurance to his readers or hearers of the persistence of the inner values of their culture." In Richler's opinion, "any serious writer is a moralist, and only incidentally an entertainer." For Lowry, "all first-rate short stories are first rate because they are essentially 'poems', they are bound together by an integrity which is essentially poetic." Still, each "may have to find out what it is from people apart from its author and be helped by various people to exist." Thus, the role of the reader is vital. "To keep on writing short stories you have to believe that there is someone out there who will someday want to read them and that what you are doing is relevant and valid." So writes David Lewis Stein, one of our writers recently over the hump of thirty. To the younger apprentices the short story equals judging oneself from outside, judging another from within. In re-presenting the human condition it offers no solutions; instead, a self-imposed particular order employing language as the filter of the flood of phenomena in which we are all carried. Poe's sailor in "A Descent into the Maelstrom" saves himself by studying the action of the whirlpool and by co-operating with it. This should be a lesson to us all, thinks McLuhan, for "we are now obliged not to attack or avoid the strom but to study its operation as providing a means of release from it". In the last analysis the short story consists of the million drops of water in which all the days of our lives are potentially mirrored.

The Creative Process

From the order and disorder of life's experiences the writer imaginatively composes a kaleidoscope for the reader. The conventional format of the old short story made the viewing as straightforward as possible by employing a strict selection of material to be presented via a "go-ahead" logical sequence. An X-ray of the new short story reveals it is a "collideorscope" of collage and montage where time and space intersect significantly and sufficiently to yield "themeanings" within an "electrick" universe. Extracting from the multiplicity of reality all the discrete fragments that concern him, the author structures his narrative on a "go-around" and "go-down" basis that circulates within the chosen borders of time and space. Thus, to the horizontally progressive format of the old short story has been added the vertical spiral of in-depth awareness that exists independent of plot. Mystery is perpendicular to language.

By the light of the author's flashes of perception the reader sees a unique presentation of facts in motion. If these flashes are bright enough, both writer and reader will be plunged into the story by the end of the first paragraph, which Robert Ruark once called the "customer-grabber". Look now at the opening paragraphs of each story for the mystery intended to catapult your curiosity onward. Here the causal factors of the story's final effect are introduced so that the actualized ending is the logical result of at least one potentiality in the story's beginning. Following the example of Poe, some writers work backwards from the effect they want on the reader to the necessary lead-up elements that will inevitably but not too openly determine the conclusion.

The problem of how much to include in a short story, quantitatively as well as qualitatively, is visible in Thomas Wolfe's statement "that a great writer is not only a leaver-outer but also a putter-inner." James Joyce has shown the twentieth century that within the medium of language—slanguage, langwedge and our daily bread slangwiches—man has collectively put in as many as three symbolic levels under the surface meaning. He once told a critic that far from being "trivial" his works were "quadrivial"! There is not much left out when our literacy includes "scientific and religious and personal and social and newspaper and airplane and technical and death and fear and economic and oddball languages" (to name a few that Dave Godfrey once cited). In thought and dialogue all characters speak that you the reader may see them. However, the words you read are not the words you will hear since the spoken word is a different medium to the written one. The internal slipstream of conscious thought is again separate in nature from uttered and outered language. The languages of man are as diversified as the media through which he communicates.

Characterization is presented foreground against the background of an "electrick" universe. The protagonist pits his powers of free election and selection against the tricks of time and space, the seemingly uncontrollable accidents of life and the jests of God, hap and fate. Since election is active, trickery passive, character motivation plays the important role in determining the positive rather than negative destinies of each of us. Motivation depends on personality, itself shaped by the interaction of physical and mental agents. Conflict, without which no story has any "themeaning", depends on the collision course of impacting mental and environmental interests. Put simply, the causal course of any character's story results from the following questions and answers intermeshing within an artistic mosaic: *who?* characters; *why?* motivation; *what?* theme; *when?* time; *where?* "splace"; *how?* plot; *which?* means. After each story ask yourself how successfully these seven important questions have been answered through the mesh-medium.

Plot carries the characters horizontally into the future while "themeaning" develops vertically from the tell-tale significances of action. Lacking the expansiveness of the novelist, the short story writer must completely exploit the isolated slice of life he has selected. Knowing that time and space are the two universal strands that splice together the vital rope of each man's life, the writer aims towards at least one "epiphany" or manifestation of self-awareness per story. Usually near its end the main character discovers himself through an "augenblick". This German word, literally meaning the flickering of an eyelid, describes that moment of the present where the past is still with him and the future already alive. Time past and time future converge in an "electrick" shock of self-cognition in the laserbeam of time present. At these "spots of time" (Wordsworth), or "stops in time" (Dylan Thomas), each man momentarily sees the naked truth of who and what he has become through his actions. The Japanese call it *satori*, the mystics *illumination*; both see that this purity of self-perception although highly personal in one light, can brighten the dark paths of other men's lives too. You the reader should not leave behind any story until you have "seen the light" for, to paraphrase André Gide, a story is always a collaboration, and the greater its value the smaller the part of the writer. As we expect all things in nature to reveal themselves, so let us expect our stories to be revealed by readers.

Each of us has a unique bias of communication or viewpoint, a means to an end which McLuhan has described as follows:

> "Interface" refers to the interaction of substances in a kind of mutual irritation. In art and poetry this is precisely the technique of "symbolism" (Greek "symballein"—to throw together) with its paratactic procedure of juxtaposing without connectives. It is the natural form of conversation or dialogue rather than of written discourse. In writing, the tendency is to isolate an aspect of some matter and to direct steady attention upon that aspect. In dialogue there is an equally natural interplay of multiple aspects of any matter. This interplay of aspects can generate insights or discovery. By contrast, a point of view is merely a way of *looking at* something. But an insight is the sudden awareness of a complex process of interaction. An insight is a contact with the life of forms. . . . "A person may spend a long while looking before recognition occurs, but when it occurs it is 'instantaneous'."

When the end of a story is in sight, the end should be *insight*, that pleasurable inner feeling of seeing into the mirror of life. Additional readings of all good stories will reward the seeker with fresh insights. Familiarity breeds content.

The Five Fingers of This Anthology

United the five stories of this anthology become a handshake welcoming you the teacher and student alike to further familiarity with the authors listed in the bibliography. Individually each story is a unique signpost testifying to the diversity of potential within the genre. "Flying a Red Kite" comes first as an example of the standard story reaching towards symbolic narrative. Naturalistic and straightforward, the "go-ahead" plot is amplified by seemingly digressive description that artfully immerses the reader in far more than the atmosphere of a hot July Montreal scene. The kite flying over the cemetery is a symbolic rebirth, a "themeaning" arrived at organically rather than artificially. "Something for Olivia's Scrapbook I Guess" is presented so casually through its conversational format that the reader is stunned by direct intimacy with an unknown narrator's deadpan storytelling. The older narrator of "The Happiest Days" is similarly unemotional in establishing a mobile concurrency between his past and present life. Not until the final epiphany does the reader discover in this vignette the full realization of the teacher's cancerous entropy. "Some Grist for Mervyn's Mill" is a far more complete study of the rise and fall of great expectations, recounted by Richler's masterful ear for the intonations, resonances and nuances of dialogue. Finally, in contrast, is the destructively introspective world of a dying writer for whom the past is both grist and foreshadowing future. Together the five fingers point to a variety of literary experiences.

Tradition and Innovation

According to Gertrude Stein, "When one is beginning to write he is always under the shadow of the thing that is just past. And that is why the creative person always has the appearance of ugliness," together with the pain-pleasure syndrome of giving birth to one's own brain-child. Why bother to experiment? Simply because the rewards justify the struggle. Future achievement of the short story in Canada depends partially on new writers seeing what has already been done badly and well, but moreso being perceptively receptive to the "land of the Now" as Sherwood Anderson once called his strange land that few had entered. "A man who is making a revolution has to be contemporary" wrote Stein. Hopefully you the teacher and student together will use these five stories not as ends in themselves, but rather as points of departure models from which to springboard your own innovations.

RECIPE FOR A SHORT STORY

>Take one strong feeling
>Add characters
>Stir with conflict
>Allow all to sizzle.

WHAT? THEME: WHO? CHARACTERS: WHY? MOTIVATION: WHEN? TIME: WHERE? "SPLACE": HOW? PLOT: WHICH? MEANS.

You are now en route to what the playwright Ionesco recently claimed to be writing's goal:

> Literature must stun, must be the stupefaction of being. . . It must be ardent, intense, primordially stunning, like a conflagration, even more powerful than the holocaust around us, stronger than our *joies de vivre*, our sorrows, and our deaths.

On the following two pages of this book, our artists have attempted to illustrate some of the terms used in discussing fiction. Can you suggest other ways or more effective ways in which these terms could be illustrated?

Some of the terms used are unusual. They have been coined by the author. Are they effective? Are they necessary? Can you suggest or compose other terms which would be helpful in discussing the modern short story?

COLLIDEORSCOPE is the all-at-once impact of collage and montage.

ELECTRICK UNIVERSE is our world where everyone's election or choice CONFLICTS with the tricks of time and space. *

TIME is the NOW through which the FUTURE plunges into the PAST

SPACE is the macrocosm within which the writer selects a microcosm.

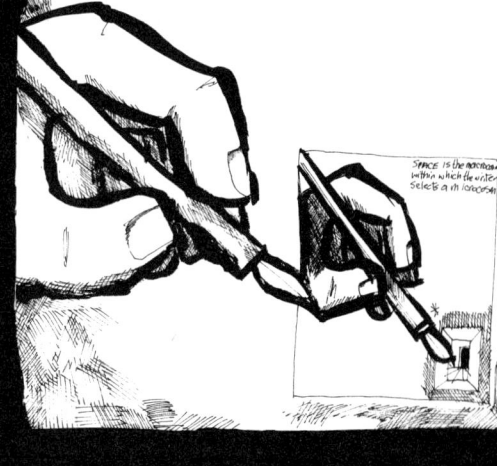

THEMEANING is any significant interpretation derived from the complexities of a story.

EPIPHANY is a symbolic moment in which people or things reveal their true characters or essences.

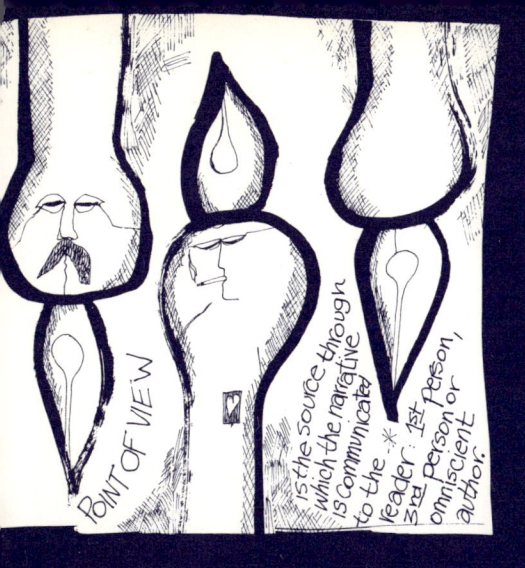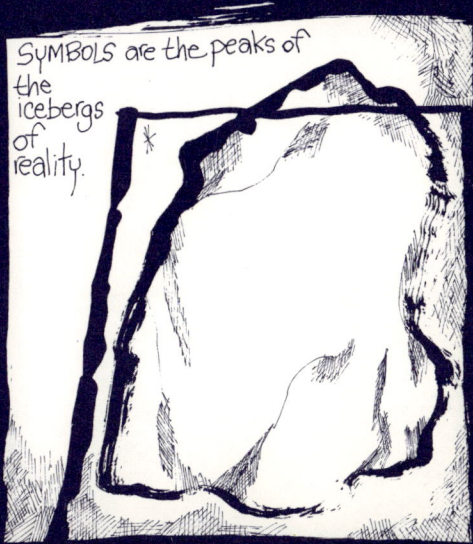

Hugh Hood

Hugh Hood (1928-) was born of a Nova Scotian father and a French-Canadian mother in Toronto. He holds three degrees from the University of Toronto and is perfectly bilingual. His first book *Flying a Red Kite* (1962) was a collection of eleven short stories; his second a collection called *Around the Mountain: Scenes from Montreal Life* (1967). He is also the author of three novels, *White Figure, White Ground* (1964), *The Camera Always Lies* (1967), *A Game of Touch* (1970), and a biography, *Strength Down Centre: The Jean Beliveau Story* (1970). He teaches English at the University of Montreal.

Sean O'Faolain, one of this century's better short story writers has described his medium as follows: "It is like a child's kite, a small wonder, a brief, bright moment. . . . if it is good, it moves in the same element as the largest work of art — up there, airborne. The main thing a writer of a short story wants to do is get it off the ground as quickly as possible, hold it up there, taut and tense, playing it like a fish." In a different medium, the fifth of Carl Sandburg's Ten Definitions of Poetry reads: "Poetry is a theorem of a yellow-silk handkerchief knotted with riddles, sealed in a balloon tied to the tail of a kite flying in a white wind against a blue sky in spring." Hood's kite also has a symbolic meaning. Emblematic of man's mortality, it represents man's potential flight into and conquest over life's elements, particularly the winds of change.

The story is told from the limited omniscient point of view of Fred's mind. His thoughts, reactions and the dialogue and actions of others as witnessed by him are the story's content. With Fred as our live camera, we follow his bus ride home with an almost cinematic accuracy. By itself the bus trip is the longest of the three parts into which Hood has divided the tale. The Balliol man and the Father are expertly sketched as though living characters drawn from real life. The Father especially disappoints Fred because he mirrors the "spoiled priest" within himself, the failure who doubts that he can even fly the kite. When, however, he does succeed he knows that he has proved the priest wrong about the "shamness" of life. He has also proved on a small scale not to be a spoiled priest.

Characterizational development within Fred is complemented by his reflection in Deedee's actions. The three-part story, traditional in its beginning, middle and end partitions, is elevated from banality by Hood's acute sense of place, a vivid eye for description and exposition, and a naturally coherent blending of narrative and exposition. Hood has written elsewhere, "landscape has no special grace in itself". Rather it is the relationship between the characters and the cityscape that endows the setting with significance. "All around me; there's a story in everybody around us.... Work for a lifetime, I said smugly. You should see my notebook. I'll never write them all."

Although the story seems to be just a simple tale told straightforwardly, compare its point of view with the camera eye behind the National Film Board's colour film of this story: *The Red Kite*, 17 minutes, (35mm 105 c 0165 117; 16mm 106 c 0165 117.) Do a detailed comparison on the differences. Also, discuss the full symbolic significance of the kites in O'Faolain, Sandburg, Hood and W. O. Mitchell's novel *The Kite* in the light of Leonard Cohen's poem, "A Kite is a Victim" from *The Spice Box of Earth* (1961):

> A kite is a victim you are sure of.
> You love it because it pulls
> gentle enough to call you master,
> strong enough to call you fool;
> because it lives
> like a desperate trained falcon
> in the high sweet air,
> and you can always haul it down
> to tame it in your drawer.
>
> A kite is a fish you have already caught

20   The Canadian Short Story

in a pool where no fish come,
so you play him carefully and long,
and hope he won't give up,
or the wind die down.

A kite is the last poem you've written,
so you give it to the wind,
but you don't let it go
until someone finds you
something else to do.

A kite is a contract of glory
that must be made with the sun,
so you make friends with the field
the river and the wind,
then you pray the whole cold night before,
under the travelling cordless moon,
to make you worthy and lyric and pure.

Flying a Red Kite

The ride home began badly. Still almost a stranger to the city, tired, hot and dirty, and inattentive to his surroundings, Fred stood for ten minutes, shifting his parcels from arm to arm and his weight from one leg to the other in a sweaty bath of shimmering glare from the sidewalk, next to a grimy yellow-and-black bus stop. To his left a line of murmuring would-be passengers lengthened until there were enough to fill any vehicle that might come for them. Finally an obese brown bus waddled up like an indecent old cow and stopped with an expiring moo at the head of the line. Fred was glad to be first in line, as there didn't seem to be room for more than a few to embus.

But as he stepped up he noticed a sign in the window which said *Côte des Neiges — Boulevard* and he recoiled as though bitten, trampling the toes of the woman behind him and making her squeal. It was a Sixty-six bus, not the Sixty-five that he wanted. The woman pushed furiously past him while the remainder of the line clamoured in the rear. He stared at the number on the bus stop: Sixty-six, not his stop at all. Out of the corner of his eye he saw another coach pulling away from the stop on the northeast corner, the right stop, the Sixty-five, and the one he should have been standing under all this time. Giving his characteristic weary put-upon sigh, which he used before breakfast to annoy Naomi, he adjusted his parcels in both arms, feeling sweat run around his neck and down his collar between his shoulders, and crossed Saint Catherine against the light, drawing a Gallic sneer from a policeman, to stand for several more minutes at the head of a new queue, under the right sign. It was nearly four-thirty and the Saturday shopping crowds wanted to get home, out of the summer dust and heat, out of the jitter of the big July holiday week-end. They would all go home and sit on their balconies. All over the suburbs in duplexes and fourplexes, families would be enjoying cold suppers in the open air on their balconies; but the Calverts' apartment had none. Fred and Naomi had been ignorant of the custom when they were apartment hunting. They had thought of Montreal as a city of the Sub-Arctic and in the summers they would have leisure to repent the misjudgment.

He had been shopping along the length of Saint Catherine between Peel and Guy, feeling guilty because he had heard for years that this was where all those pretty Montreal women made their promenade; he had wanted to watch without familial encumbrances. There had been girls enough but nothing outrageously special so he had beguiled the scorching afternoon making a great many small idle purchases, of the kind one does when trapped in a Woolworth's. A ball-point pen and a notepad for Naomi, who was always stealing his and leaving it in the kitchen with long, wildly optimistic, grocery lists scribbled in it. Six packages of cigarettes, some legal-size envelopes, two Dinky-toys, a long-playing record, two parcels of second-hand books, and the lightest of his burdens and the unhandiest, the kite he had bought for Deedee, two flimsy wooden sticks rolled up in red plastic film, and a ball of cheap thin string — not enough, by the look of it, if he should ever get the thing into the air.

When he'd gone fishing, as a boy, he'd never caught any fish; when playing hockey he had never been able to put the puck in the net. One by one the wholesome outdoor sports and games had defeated him. But he had gone on believing in them, in their curative moral values, and now he hoped that Deedee, though a girl, might sometime catch a fish; and though she obviously wouldn't play hockey, she might ski, or toboggan on the mountain. He had noticed that people treated kites and kite-flying as somehow holy. They were a natural symbol, thought Fred, and he felt uneasily sure that he would have trouble getting this one to fly.

The inside of the bus was shaped like a box-car with windows, but the windows were useless. You might have peeled off the bus as you'd peel the paper off a pound of butter, leaving an oblong yellow lump of thick solid heat, with the passengers embedded in it like hopeless bread-crumbs.

He elbowed and wriggled his way along the aisle, feeling a momentary sliver of pleasure as his palm rubbed accidentally along the back of a girl's skirt — once, a philosopher — the sort of thing you couldn't be charged with. But you couldn't get away with it twice and anyway the girl either didn't feel it, or had no idea who had caressed her. There were vacant seats towards the rear, which was odd because the bus was otherwise full, and he struggled towards them, trying not to break the wooden struts which might be

Flying A Red Kite 23

persuaded to fly. The bus lurched forward and his feet moved with the floor, causing him to pop suddenly out of the crowd by the exit, into a square well of space next to the heat and stink of the engine. He swayed around and aimed himself at a narrow vacant seat, nearly dropping a parcel of books as he lowered himself precipitately into it.

The bus crossed Sherbrooke Street and began, intolerably slowly, to crawl up Côte des Neiges and around the western spur of the mountain. His ears began to pick up the usual mélange of French and English and to sort it out; he was proud of his French and pleased that most of the people on the streets spoke a less correct, though more fluent, version than his own. He had found that he could make his customers understand him perfectly — he was a book salesman — but that people on the street were happier when he addressed them in English.

The chatter in the bus grew clearer and more interesting and he began to listen, grasping all at once why he had found a seat back here. He was sitting next to a couple of drunks who emitted an almost overpowering smell of beer. They were cheerfully exchanging indecencies and obscure jokes and in a minute they would speak to him. They always did, drunks and panhandlers, finding some soft fearfulness in his face which exposed him as a shrinking easy mark. Once in a railroad station he had been approached three times in twenty minutes by the same panhandler on his rounds. Each time he had given the man something, despising himself with each new weakness.

The cheerful pair sitting at right-angles to him grew louder and more blunt and the women within earshot grew glum. There was no harm in it; there never is. But you avoid your neighbour's eye, afraid of smiling awkwardly, or of looking offended and a prude.

"Now this Pearson," said one of the revellers, "he's just a little short-ass. He's just a little fellow without any brains. Why, some of the speeches he makes . . . I could make them myself. I'm an old Tory myself, an old Tory."

"I'm an old Blue," said the other.

"Is that so, now? That's fine, a fine thing." Fred was sure he didn't know what a Blue was.

"I'm a Balliol man. Whoops!" They began to make monkey-like noises to annoy the passengers and amuse themselves. "Whoops," said the Oxford man again, "hoo, hoo, there's one now, there's one for you." He was talking about a girl on the sidewalk.

"She's one, now, isn't she? Look at the legs on her, oh, look at them now, isn't that something?" There was a noisy clearing of throats and the same voice said something that sounded like "Shaoil-na-baig."

"Oh, good, good!" said the Balliol man.

"Shaoil-na-baig," said the other loudly, "I've not forgotten my Gaelic, do you see, shaoil-na-baig," he said it loudly, and a woman up the aisle reddened and looked away. It sounded like a dirty phrase to Fred, delivered as though the speaker had forgotten all his Gaelic but the words for sexual intercourse.

"And how is your French, Father?" asked the Balliol man, and the title made Fred start in his seat. He pretended to drop a parcel and craned his head quickly sideways. The older of the two drunks, the one sitting by the window, examining the passing legs and skirts with the same impulse that Fred had felt on Saint Catherine Street, was indeed a priest, and couldn't possibly be an imposter. His clerical suit was too well-worn, egg-stained and blemished with candle-droppings, and fit its wearer too well, for it to be an assumed costume. The face was unmistakably a southern Irishman's. The priest darted a quick peek into Fred's eyes before he could turn them away, giving a monkey-like grimace that might have been a mixture of embarrassment and shame but probably wasn't.

He was a little grey-haired bucko of close to sixty, with a triangular sly mottled crimson face and uneven yellow teeth. His hands moved jerkily and expressively in his lap, in counterpoint to the lively intelligent movements of his face.

The other chap, the Balliol man, was a perfect type of English-speaking Montrealer, perhaps a bond salesman or minor functionary in a brokerage house on Saint James Street. He was about fifty with a round domed head, red hair beginning to go slightly white at the neck and ears, pink porcine skin, very neatly barbered and combed. He wore an expensive white shirt with a fine blue stripe and there was some sort of ring around his tie. He had his hands folded flatly on the knob of a stick, round face with deep laugh-lines in the cheeks, and a pair of cheerfully darting little blue bloodshot eyes. Where could the pair have run into each other?

Flying A Red Kite

"I've forgotten my French years ago," said the priest carelessly. "I was down in New Brunswick for many years and I'd no use for it, the work I was doing. I'm Irish, you know."

"I'm an old Blue."

"That's right," said the priest, "John's the boy. Oh, he's a sharp lad is John. He'll let them all get off, do you see, to Manitoba for the summer, and bang, BANG!" All the bus jumped. "He'll call an election on them and then they'll run." Something caught his eye and he turned to gaze out the window. The bus was moving slowly past the cemetery of Notre Dame des Neiges and the priest stared, half-sober, at the graves stretched up the mountainside in the sun.

"I'm not in there," he said involuntarily.

"Indeed you're not," said his companion, "lot's of life in you yet, eh, Father?"

"Oh," he said, "oh, I don't think I'd know what to do with a girl if I fell over one." He looked out at the cemetery for several moments. "It's all a sham," he said, half under his breath, "they're in there for good." He swung around and looked innocently at Fred. "Are you going fishing, lad?"

"It's a kite that I bought for my little girl," said Fred, more cheerfully than he felt.

"She'll enjoy that, she will," said the priest, "for it's grand sport."

"Go fly a kite!" said the Oxford man hilariously. It amused him and he said it again. "Go fly a kite!" He and the priest began to chant together, "Hoo, hoo, whoops," and they laughed and in a moment, clearly, would begin to sing.

The bus turned lumberingly onto Queen Mary Road. Fred stood up confusedly and began to push his way towards the rear door. As he turned away, the priest grinned impudently at him, stammering a jolly goodbye. Fred was too embarrassed to answer but he smiled uncertainly and fled. He heard them take up their chant anew.

"Ho, there's one for you, hoo. Shaoil-na-baig. Whoops!" Their laughter died out as the bus rolled heavily away.

He had heard about such men, naturally, and knew that they existed; but it was the first time in Fred's life that he had ever seen a priest misbehave himself publicly. There are so many priests

26   *The Canadian Short Story*

in the city, he thought, that the number of bum ones must be in proportion. The explanation satisfied him but the incident left a disagreeable impression in his mind.

Safely home he took his shirt off and poured himself a Coke. Then he allowed Deedee, who was dancing around him with her terrible energy, to open the parcels.

"Give your Mummy the pad and pencil, sweetie," he directed. She crossed obediently to Naomi's chair and handed her the cheap plastic case.

"Let me see you make a note in it," he said, "make a list of something, for God's sake, so you'll remember it's yours. And the one on the desk is mine. Got that?" He spoke without rancour or much interest; it was a rather overworked joke between them.

"What's this?" said Deedee, holding up the kite and allowing the ball of string to roll down the hall. He resisted a compulsive wish to get up and re-wind the string.

"It's for you. Don't you know what it is?"

"It's a red kite," she said. She had wanted one for weeks but spoke now as if she weren't interested. Then all at once she grew very excited and eager. "Can you put it together right now?" she begged.

"I think we'll wait till after supper, sweetheart," he said, feeling mean. You raised their hopes and then dashed them; there was no real reason why they shouldn't put it together now, except his fatigue. He looked pleadingly at Naomi.

"Daddy's tired, Deedee," she said obligingly, "he's had a long hot afternoon."

"But I want to see it," said Deedee, fiddling with the flimsy red film and nearly puncturing it.

Fred was sorry he'd drunk a Coke; it bloated him and upset his stomach and had no true cooling effect.

"We'll have something to eat," he said cajolingly, "and then Mummy can put it together for you." He turned to his wife. "You don't mind, do you? I'd only spoil the thing." Threading a needle or hanging a picture made the normal slight tremor of his hands accentuate itself almost embarrassingly.

"Of course not," she said, smiling wryly. They had long ago worked out their areas of uselessness.

Flying A Red Kite 27

"There's a picture on it, and directions."

"Yes. Well, we'll get it together somehow. Flying it . . . that's something else again." She got up, holding the note-pad, and went into the kitchen to put the supper on.

It was a good hot-weather supper, tossed greens with the correct proportions of vinegar and oil, croissants and butter, and cold sliced ham. As he ate, his spirits began to percolate a bit, and he gave Naomi a graphic sketch of the incident on the bus. "It depressed me," he told her. This came as no surprise to her; almost anything unusual, which he couldn't do anything to alter or relieve, depressed Fred nowadays. "He must have been sixty. Oh, quite sixty. I should think, and you could tell that everything had come to pieces for him."

"It's a standard story," she said, "and aren't you sentimentalizing it?"

"In what way?"

"The 'spoiled priest' business, the empty man, the man without a calling. They all write about that. Graham Greene made his whole career out of that."

"That isn't what the phrase means," said Fred laboriously. "It doesn't refer to a man who actually *is* a priest, though without a vocation."

"No?" She lifted an eyebrow; she was better educated than he.

"No, it doesn't. It means somebody who never became a priest at all. The point is that you *had* a vocation but ignored it. That's what a spoiled priest is. It's an Irish phrase, and usually refers to somebody who is a failure and who drinks too much." He laughed shortly. "I don't qualify, on the second count."

"You're not a failure."

"No, I'm too young. Give me time!" There was no reason for him to talk like this; he was a very productive salesman.

"You certainly never wanted to be a priest," she said positively, looking down at her breasts and laughing, thinking of some secret. "I'll bet you never considered it, not with your habits." She meant his bedroom habits, which were ardent, and in which she ardently acquiesced. She was an adept and enthusiastic partner, her greatest gift as a wife.

"Let's put that kite together," said Deedee, getting up from her little table, with such adult decision that her parents chuckled.

"Come on," she said, going to the sofa and bouncing up and down.

Naomi put a tear in the fabric right away, on account of the ambiguity of the directions. There should have been two holes in the kite, through which a lugging-string passed; but the holes hadn't been provided and when she put them there with the point of an icepick they immediately began to grow.

"Scotch tape," she said, like a surgeon asking for sutures.

"There's a picture on the front," said Fred, secretly cross but ostensibly helpful.

"I see it," she said.

"Mummy put holes in the kite," said Deedee with alarm. "Is she going to break it?"

"No," said Fred. The directions were certainly ambiguous.

Naomi tied the struts at right-angles, using so much string that Fred was sure the kite would be too heavy. Then she strung the fabric on the notched ends of the struts and the thing began to take shape.

"It doesn't look quite right," she said, puzzled and irritated.

"The surface has to be curved so there's a difference of air pressure." He remembered this, rather unfairly, from high school physics classes.

She bent over the cross-piece and tied it in a bowed arc, and the red film pulled taut. "There now," she said.

"You've forgotten the lugging-string on the front," said Fred critically, "that's what you made the holes for, remember?"

"Why is Daddy mad?" said Deedee.

"I'M NOT MAD!"

It had begun to shower, great pear-shaped drops of rain falling with a plop on the sidewalk.

"That's as close as I can come," said Naomi, staring at Fred, "we aren't going to try it tonight, are we?"

"We promised her," he said, "and it's only a light rain."

"Will we all go?"

"I wish you'd take her," he said, "because my stomach feels upset. I should never drink Coca-Cola."

"It always bothers you. You should know that by now."

"I'm not running out on you," he said anxiously, "and if you can't make it work, I'll take her up tomorrow afternoon."

Flying A Red Kite 29

"I know," she said, "come on, Deedee, we're going to take the kite up the hill." They left the house and crossed the street. Fred watched them through the window as they started up the steep path hand in hand. He felt left out and slightly nauseated.

They were back in half an hour, their spirits not at all dampened, which surprised him.

"No go, eh?"

"Much too wet, and not enough breeze. The rain knocks it flat."

"O.K.!" he exclaimed with fervour. "I'll try tomorrow."

"We'll try again tomorrow," said Deedee with equal determination — her parents mustn't forget their obligations.

Sunday afternoon the weather was nearly perfect, hot, clear, a firm steady breeze but not too much of it, and a cloudless sky. At two o'clock Fred took his daughter by the hand and they started up the mountain together, taking the path through the woods that led up to the University parking lots.

"We won't come down until we make it fly," Fred swore, "that's a promise."

"Good," she said, hanging on to his hand and letting him drag her up the steep path, "there are lots of bugs in here, aren't there?"

"Yes," he said briefly — he was being liberally bitten.

When they came to the end of the path, they saw that the campus was deserted and still, and there was all kinds of running room. Fred gave Deedee careful instructions about where to sit, and what to do if a car should come along, and then he paid out a little string and began to run across the parking lot towards the main building of the University. He felt a tug at the string and throwing a glance over his shoulder he saw the kite bobbing in the air, about twenty feet off the ground. He let out more string, trying to keep it filled with air, but he couldn't run quite fast enough, and in a moment it fell back to the ground.

"Nearly had it!" he shouted to Deedee, whom he'd left fifty yards behind.

"Daddy, Daddy, come back," she hollered apprehensively. Rolling up the string as he went, he retraced his steps and prepared to try again. It was important to catch a gust of wind and run into it. On the second try the kite went higher than before but as he ran past the entrance to the University he felt the air pressure lapse and saw the kite waver and fall. He walked slowly back, realizing that the bulk of the main building was cutting off the air currents.

"We'll go up higher," he told her, and she seized his hand and climbed obediently up the road beside him, around behind the main building, past ash barrels and trash heaps; they climbed a flight of wooden steps, crossed a parking lot next to L'Ecole Polytechnique and a slanting field further up, and at last came to a pebbly dirt road that ran along the top ridge of the mountain beside the cemetery. Fred remembered the priest as he looked across the fence and along the broad stretch of cemetery land rolling away down the slope of the mountain to the west. They were about six hundred feet above the river, he judged. He'd never been up this far before.

"My sturdy little brown legs are tired," Deedee remarked, and he burst out laughing.

"Where did you hear that," he said, "who has sturdy little brown legs?"

She screwed her face up in a grin. "The gingerbread man," she said, beginning to sing, "I can run away from you, I can, 'cause I'm the little gingerbread man."

The air was dry and clear and without a trace of humidity and the sunshine was dazzling. On either side of the dirt road grew great clumps of wildflowers, yellow and blue, buttercups, daisies and goldenrod, and cornflowers and clover. Deedee disappeared into the flowers — picking bouquets was her favourite game. He could see the shrubs and grasses heave and sway as she moved around. The scent of clover and of dry sweet grass was very keen here, and from the east, over the curved top of the mountain, the wind blew in a steady uneddying stream. Five or six miles off to the southwest, he spied the wide intensely grey-white stripe of the river. He heard Deedee cry: "Daddy, Daddy, come and look." He pushed through the coarse grasses and found her.

"Berries," she cried rapturously, "look at all the berries! Can I eat them?" She had found a wild raspberry bush, a thing he hadn't seen since he was six years old. He'd never expected to find one growing in the middle of Montreal.

Flying A Red Kite 31

"Wild raspberries," he said wonderingly, "sure you can pick them dear; but be careful of the prickles." They were all shades and degrees of ripeness from black to vermilion.

"Ouch," said Deedee, pricking her finger as she pulled off the berries. She put a handful in her mouth and looked wry.

"Are they bitter?"

"Juicy," she mumbled with her mouth full. A trickle of dark juice ran down her chin.

"Eat some more," he said, "while I try the kite again." She bent absorbedly to the task of hunting them out, and he walked down the road for some distance and then turned to run up towards her. This time he gave the kite plenty of string before he began to move; he ran as hard as he could, panting and handing the string out over his shoulders, burning his fingers as it slid through them. All at once he felt the line pull and pulse as if there were a living thing on the other end and he turned on his heel and watched while the kite danced into the upper air-currents above the treetops and began to soar up and up. He gave it more line and in an instant it pulled high up away from him across the fence, two hundred feet and more above him up over the cemetery where it steadied and hung, bright red in the sunshine. He thought flashingly of the priest saying "It's all a sham," and he knew all at once that the priest was wrong. Deedee came running down to him, laughing with excitement and pleasure and singing joyfully about the gingerbread man, and he knelt in the dusty roadway and put his arms around her, placing her hands on the line between his. They gazed, squinting in the sun, at the flying red thing, and he turned away and saw in the shadow of her cheek and on her lips and chin the dark rich red of the pulp and juice of the crushed raspberries.

David Helwig

David Helwig (1938-) was born in Toronto and raised there and in Niagara-on-the-Lake. In 1968 he published *Figures in a Landscape*, a book of poems; in 1969 *The Streets of Summer* from which this story is taken. He teaches English at Queen's University.

The casual offhandedness of the title prepares one for an indifferent narrative approach. True to form the droning equitone of Olivia's husband admits us to an impersonal view of that which should be highly personal, namely intimate relationships. Slowly, with his eye as the first circle and the horizon which it forms as the second, the narrator's viewpoint is coolly detached as in retrospect he relives the series of events which has mysteriously altered his concept of love. Jealousy, lust, and promiscuity are startlingly sublimated to the nobler concept of sacrifice without the narrator's awareness of how the change occurred. Just how the theme switches from hedonism to Samaritanism should be carefully investigated.

At first glance the nameless Barrow Man appears to be another type of Harold Bettmann. His inexplicable charisma tantalizes women who as a result find him irresistible. Initially his dominating nature makes no exception of the little deaf mute; a satyr, his aim is just to make her happy sexually, sooner or later. When Jane talks him out of seducing her he simply substitutes Jane as his prey. "Universally accommodating" Jane becomes a partner in Barrow Man's "missionary zeal". Suddenly, contrary to Mary McCarthy's belief that "Sex annihilates identity, and the space given to sex in contemporary novels is an avowal of the absence of character", Jane, Barrow Man and the narrator display an altruism unsuspected in them until now.

The entire story hinges on this "rising to the occasion" of self-sacrifice. All of the characters except Olivia unite to forget temporarily their "belly gods". But why? Can you account for the individual motivation behind each of the deaf mute's "helpers"? What aspects of the "electrick" universe are visible in a setting where manipulation has been the customary substitute for communication? Helwig has carefully eliminated any false thematic exposition so that you and the narrator alike are left at the end saying "don't start asking me why". Is the ending satisfactory to you? Compare it with the ending of Hood's story as an affirmation of the life-force that is always threatened with extinction in the lives of boxed-in people.

The film *Flowers on a One-Way Street* (National Film Board, 1967, 57 minutes) depicts a clash between the Yorkville hippies and the City Fathers. Compare this confrontation with that in Helwig's story.

Something for Olivia's Scrapbook I Guess

I was alone in the shop as I watched the two of them coming up the street. Olivia was on television being interviewed with a discovery, Harold Bettmann, "one of the most exciting young sculptors working in Canada today" (*Toronto Star*). I felt a bit sorry for Olivia over the Harold thing. He is not a nice young man, and to a bystander he seems too obviously to be trying to reach the top of the mountain of success by a route beginning with a tunnel into my wife's private parts. Still, I knew better than to say anything to her. Anyway, they were on television together, and I certainly wasn't going to watch. So I stood in the front window and watched Barrow Man and the girl.

I wasn't really surprised to see her tagging along after Barrow Man as he came up the street. Women can smell it on him, I've often observed that. My wife for example: when Barrow Man walks into a room she shuts her mouth and sits very still licking her lips now and then. And that's about the only time she stops talking. You wouldn't think there'd be any mystery about him; at least a couple of times I've heard him going out the back door as I came in the front, but still, when he comes into a room, Olivia shuts her gob and sits with that funny look on her face. No-one else does that to her, and there are lots better-looking than Barrow Man, more charming, more intelligent. But women like him. They look at that bony face and that thick hair, and they smell whatever it is he has and bingo. So I wasn't surprised to see this young girl following him along the street as he pushed his barrow of tatty flowers along.

Our place is just north of Yorkville, where Yorkville is going to expand next, that's what the real-estate man says. Anyway Olivia and I have a shop there, full of handicrafts and imported odds and ends that nobody buys. Barrow Man lives next door with a gang of others in rooms upstairs from something that's trying to be a coffee house.

Barrow Man is unscrupulous, have I established that? Suppose not. Well he is, but just about women, just about sex really. I've seen him fill a fifteen-year-old with wine and take her upstairs without even paying much attention to who she is. He thinks it's good for them, that's the secret, and otherwise he's kind and generous. Only for him it's not an otherwise. He thinks that sex is good for any woman at any time and any place whether she thinks so or not. Maybe he's right. Maybe that's what women see in him.

So as I say, I wasn't surprised that afternoon when I saw the girl following Barrow Man up the street. He'd been down at his usual spot on Cumberland selling flowers that he'd picked from parks and gardens the night before or got from florists who were ready to throw them out. Flowers have been getting a lot of publicity this year, and he sold them cheap and made enough to stay alive.

The girl who was following him up the street was dressed in clothes that were worn almost to tatters and were too big for her. Every few feet she would stop. It seemed as though Barrow Man could hear when her feet stopped moving, for he would turn around almost immediately and motion to her with his hand. Gradually she would get up her courage and move forward a few feet. It took them five or ten minutes to cross the distance between the point where I first saw them and the house. Barrow Man's missionary zeal amazed me. To go to all this trouble when he could have half a dozen women in the neighbourhood for the asking. Jane, whose room was right next to his, was an attractive and universally accommodating girl.

When they reached the front of the house, Barrow Man made an elaborate gesture indicating that he lived there and inviting the girl to sit at one of the outside tables. It was then I caught on that she must be a deaf mute. From the way she was dressed, you'd think he'd picked her up at the Salvation Army or an orphange somewhere. She sat down at one of the tables and Barrow Man disappeared inside.

The girl had a strange flat frightened face that looked straight ahead and gave the impression that she was waiting for some kind of blow to fall on her from behind. Call me sentimental, but I didn't much like the idea of Barrow Man screwing this pathetic little deaf mute.

He came out of the house with a lemonade for her and put it on the table. She didn't want to touch it in a way, but she was probably hot and thirsty and needed it. Barrow Man kept after her and she finally took a drink. While she was drinking, Barrow Man went over to the barrow of flowers that he had left at the curb and took out a handful of zinnias that he must have got from somebody's garden. He carried them over to the girl and gave them to her. I had to admire his technique.

I walked out of the shop and along the pavement toward the two of them. Just as I got to the barrow of flowers, I thought of a way to neutralize what he'd done. I took a bunch of chrysanthemums, a little wilted and obviously second-hand, and carried them over to the girl. She was holding the gaudy zinnias in her hand, and she didn't move or object when I began to put the chrysanthemums in her hair. The hair was full of tats so it was easy to find places to stick the flowers. It was soft too and reminded me of the days when Olivia's hair was brown.

Two kids about sixteen, a boy and girl who had the room across from Jane but hardly ever came out, had seen us from the window and appeared from the house. They'd lived there for weeks, but this was only the second time I'd seen them. They joined in the game, running to get flowers and carrying them to the table. They put them on the girl or placed them around her. Jane was looking out the upstairs window and threw me a couple of paper flowers from her room. I wound the wire stems around the girl's wrists. Within a few minutes, the barrow was stripped of all its flowers, which now covered the girl, the chair she sat in and the table in front of her. She made a lovely funeral. The four of us and Jane, who had come downstairs, and even Walter who had come out of the shop, stood and admired her. Barrow Man tried to get her to smile and finally she did. She seemed to relax a little and looked at the flowers, for the first time really.

"Who is she?" It was one of the young kids that asked.

"I don't know who she is," Barrow Man said. "She was hanging around near my stand all afternoon."

"What are you going to do with her?" I said.

"Well, right now," he said, "she looks so gorgeous I wouldn't dare touch her."

"Maybe you should take it a bit easy."

"What do you think I am? I'm full of loving kindness. I sell flowers and make people happy. I let you crazy people steal every

Olivia's Scrapbook 37

one of my flowers to give her. I just want to make her happy."

"But not everyone has the same idea of what will make her happy," Jane said.

"You mean sex," Barrow Man said. "You're all against sex. What a lot of nervous people you must be." He walked over to the girl, picked up her hand, and kissed the back of it.

"I'm hungry," he said, "and I suppose she is too. Some of you nervous people who stole my flowers should buy us something to eat."

"Get them some food, Walter," I said, "I'll pay."

It was after six, so I went home, closed the shop and made myself a sandwich. I planned to go back next door, but I can't afford to eat at Walter's prices. With my sandwich I had a couple of stiff drinks of rye and water which didn't do anything very metaphysical to me. I went back over to see what was happening next door, taking the bottle with me in a paper bag. The fuzz is very active around our streets.

The girl was still sitting at her table with Barrow Man and was still covered with flowers. She had drawn a bit of a crowd from the houses nearby, and Walter was doing some business for a change. I paid him for what Barrow Man and the girl had eaten and sat down at the table with them. I poured out my bag into a coffee cup and gave Barrow Man some too.

I looked at the girl. She seemed pretty puzzled but not too unhappy about the whole thing. The boy from upstairs had apparently decided to rejoin society and brought out a guitar. People started singing. That worried Walter, who was sure it would cost him his licence and invited everybody inside. When he got in the place was so crowded that Barrow Man locked the front door and put up a Closed sign. Walter pulled the curtains shut, and I took my bottle out of its paper bag. The deaf mute sat in the middle of the room in her flowers, apparently puzzled by what was going on, but everyone smiled and gestured at her, and she got used to it. I offered her a drink, but she smelled it and made a face. Walter put some music on his record player and several people formed a circle and danced around the girl. I didn't feel like dancing and concentrated on my whisky.

I finally drank enough to lose track of time, and from that point on, the party was a series of moments in a sea of noise.

First moment: someone gave her a pencil and paper, and she wrote one word. JESUS. In large scrawled capitals.

Second moment: at Jane's urging, Barrow Man publicly announced that he would not seduce the deaf mute. He called it a sentimental gesture.

Third moment: the unknown girl from upstairs began a beautifully graceful and sinuous dance.

I watched her for about twenty seconds before I decided that I couldn't take it. I went out the back door, climbed over the fence and into my yard. I stood among the few blades of brown grass that flourish there. The house was dark and I didn't want to go in. Did go in. The memory of that girl covered with flowers got to me and made me want to do something for her, not that there was anything to do.

I was making my breakfast the next morning when I heard Olivia come in. I looked at the clock. It was quarter after eight. I couldn't really figure out why she'd got up so early, didn't occur to me until she walked into the bedroom and started to undress that she hadn't been to bed. We've only got a couple of small rooms at the back of the shop, and from where I was standing, I could see her undressing. I watched. I think of it as one of my conjugal rights, although it's not really much of a sight. Olivia is a skinny little thing with no breasts to speak of and pathetic little hips. She looked so pale and dragged out as she took off her clothes that I fought off the temptation to say something witty about the long interview.

"Do you want some food?" is what I said.

She shook her head and climbed into bed. One way or another Harold must have given her a rough time. When I walked into the bedroom, she turned her face away.

"You missed a new arrival last night," I said, "Barrow Man found a strange little deaf mute somewhere. I don't know why, but everyone got excited when she turned up and gave her a big party. Even Barrow Man got into the act; he promised to refrain from debauching her. At least for the time being. It was all very strange."

She turned over and looked at me. That's not really the right way to describe it; she stared at me as though something particularly distasteful was happening on my face.

Olivia's Scrapbook 39

"Don't you ever read the newspapers?" she said.

In the circumstances, that struck me as a strange question, and I didn't answer it. After all, we'd been married nine years and she knew my reading habits. Pretty clearly it was a smart crack, but its relevance escaped me.

"She's a deaf mute about seventeen wearing old clothes that don't fit properly," Olivia said.

I nodded.

"The police are looking for her. She stabbed her mother to death with an ice pick in some little town in Muskoka and then hitch-hiked to Toronto before anyone found the body. The story was in the paper this morning and on television last night."

I thought for a few seconds and started out of the room.

"Are you going to phone the police?" she said.

"No. I'm going to warn Barrow Man that they're after her so he can hide her somewhere."

"Are you out of your mind?" As she said this, she sat up in bed, the sheet falling off her and exposing her scrawny chest. For some crazy reason, I wanted her right at that moment, but I've developed a strong resistance to such impulses and I conquered this one. At least temporarily. She went on shouting at me.

"Why in the name of all that's wonderful are you going to try to keep her away from the police? Apparently her mother drank and beat her. They'll just send her someplace where she can be looked after."

"Some nice place like the bug house."

"I don't know, but I know you have no business interfering. Just phone the police and tell them where she is, and they'll look after her all right. You're getting as crazy as those kids next door. Have they been giving you marijuana or something?"

"You know, Olivia," I said in my best Cary Grant manner, "I find your shrill grating soprano very sexy."

She got the message and covered herself with the sheet.

"You're not really going to keep her away from the police are you?"

"Unless you distract me in your subtle feminine way, I'm going to see Barrow Man right now."

She flopped down in bed.

"I should have you committed," she muttered.

"And a very Merry Christmas to you too," I said and walked down the hall and out. As I walked up to the door of the place next to us, Walter was putting out the table and chairs. He said Barrow Man was still in bed, and that the girl was in Jane's room.

I went upstairs and walked into Barrow Man's room. Jane sat up bleary-eyed in the bed and said hello.

I apologized.

"All right," Jane said. "Nothing going on. You want Barrow Man?"

"Yeah."

She reached out and shook him.

"Do you have a cigarette?" she said.

I shook my head, and she gave Barrow Man another poke. Jane, like Olivia, was sitting in bed naked down to where the sheet covered her. She is an ample girl and as I stood there, I drew certain comparisons between her and my wife. Jane poked Barrow Man twice more, and he began to make noises. Another hard poke in the ribs and he turned over.

"What's the matter?" he said.

"Olivia tells me our little friend is wanted by the police. She did in her mother with an ice pick."

"The old lady probably deserved it. Anyway, Olivia's a liar isn't she?"

"Don't really know. She says it's in the paper."

"Everything in the paper is a lie."

"What will they do to her if they find her?" Jane said.

"Put her on trial. Send her to some kind of institution."

"Nasty," Barrow Man said.

"Poor thing," Jane said. For some reason that prompted her to cover herself with the sheet. I refrained from asking why.

"What shall we do with her?" Barrow Man said.

"Turn her in or hide her," I said.

Barrow Man scratched his head.

"Don't suppose you have a cigarette."

I shook my head.

"We can't just turn her in," Jane said. "I'd feel like a judas if we did. After last night."

"Of course we didn't know last night," I said.

"Doesn't make any difference," Barrow Man said.

"No," I said, "it doesn't."

"Let's hide her somewhere," Jane said.

"Where?" Barrow Man said. "The fuzz will be watching the streets pretty carefully."

"We could put her in our back shed until tonight," I said.

"Maybe no need," Barrow Man said. "Just keep her in the house and if the fuzz shows up slip her out to your back shed."

"I wonder if she knows they're after her?" Jane said.

"She can probably guess," I said, "if she really did go at her old lady with an ice pick."

"Let's go and see her," Jane said. She climbed out of bed, stood there naked without embarrassment, stretched and put on a short cotton dress that she found on the floor beside the bed. Barrow Man pulled on a pair of pants and we went down the hall to the next door. Jane lifted her hand to knock, realized there wasn't much point, and stuck her head in. She opened the door and walked in. We followed her.

The girl was sitting on the floor at the far side of the room. She looked terrified as we walked in, and I wondered why. There was a strange unpleasant smell in the room, but it didn't much surprise me. Jane always looks a bit dirty. The girl was staring straight ahead.

"Oh my god," Jane said, "She's not housebroken."

She pointed to the other corner of the room, at a brown lump that was unmistakably the source of the smell. I looked back at the girl who was hiding her face in her skirt.

"Look," I said, "she's worried about it. I guess she didn't know where to go."

Barrow Man went over to her and lifted her face. He tried to indicate to her that it was all right, that we didn't care about the mess in the corner and that Jane would clean it up right away. Jane got a little cardboard box and did. She took it away to dispose of. Meanwhile Barrow Man started another little pantomime, asking her if she had been hitch-hiking. She nodded.

"How in hell can I ask her if she knows the cops are after her?"

"Try a traffic cop," I said, "or a motorcycle."

Barrow Man had a go at it, but the girl looked confused. Barrow Man patted her on the head and sat down. Jane walked into the room. I jumped from my chair and attacked her with an imaginary icepick. She didn't look very surprised, for she has believed for some time that I am a man full of suppressed vices. She believes this because I have never tried to make her, in spite of numerous opportunities and substantial provocation. After I had finished with Jane I turned to the girl. She looked sick. I pointed to her and nodded my head. She buried her face in her skirt again.

"Oh well," I said, "I thought we might find out something."

"Looks to me as though she did it," Jane said.

"Maybe," I said.

"I'll take her down to get some breakfast," Jane said.

Barrow Man stood up.

"Keep her in your room today. I'm going to try and find some flowers to sell. If the cops show up, put her in that back shed."

Jane took the girl by the arm and led her downstairs. I followed them to the bottom of the stairs, then turned down the hall toward the front door. On my way, I ran into Walter, who was looking worried as usual.

"You getting much business these days?" he said.

"The usual."

"I don't know how long I can hold out. I've got to eat."

"Belly god," I said and walked back to my own house of sorrows.

It was almost nine and I left the door of the shop unlocked and walked back to the kitchen. Olivia was asleep in the bedroom beside me, but something made me think she'd been up after I left. My sense of smell is sometimes very acute. She'd probably phoned the police.

I put on the kettle to make some coffee and stood in the doorway, looking in at her. She dyes her hair a colour they call champagne and it was all wild and fluffy around the little face that looked weak and pinched like that of an undernourished child.

When I had made my coffee, I took it into the shop, closed the door to the kitchen behind me and sat down at my work table near the front door. To amuse myself. I did the week's disastrous arithmetic.

It was less than half an hour after I sat down at my work table that I looked out the window and saw a police car pull up next door. I got up and ran to the back door, climbed over the low fence that separates the yards, nipped in the kitchen door and up the back stairs. As I crossed the kitchen, I could see down the hall to where the cops were coming in the front door. There were two of them, big uniformed public servants with thick necks, and at that moment, it seemed to me that I was even crazier than Olivia gave me credit for being. But my mother died in a particularly nasty government institution (a fact I have never told Olivia) and I didn't want to see this little girl put away under the thumb of some dykey matron or frustrated social worker. I grew up with social workers.

When I got to the upstairs hall, I ran as quickly as I could to Jane's room and opened the door. The girl stared at me, frightened as a bird. I gestured to her to come with me, but she didn't move. She probably didn't trust me since I had ice-picked Jane. I tried to take her arm. No dice. I ran next door to Barrow Man's room to see if Jane was there, but the room was empty. Downstairs I could hear the voices of Walter and the cops, and I knew that Walter would give her up as soon as sneeze if that was the way to avoid trouble. He had given a hostage to Fortune when he opened the coffee house, and Fortune was getting pretty good mileage out of it.

I went back into the room, spent three seconds trying to calm the girl, then picked her up and carried her along the hall and down the back stairs.

My physical condition is not outstanding. By the time we got to the kitchen, I was dizzy and thought I'd faint before I could get the girl out of there. She wasn't quite fighting me off, but she wasn't making it easy either. But for a change I got a lucky break. Jane came into the hall and into the kitchen.

"The cops are out there," she whispered.

"I know. I'm trying to get her out into our back shed, but she's afraid of me."

Jane reached out to the girl and took her hand. Girl looked a little relieved. We all slipped out the back door and over the fence. When I finally got the lock on the back shed undone, the girl refused to go in until Jane went with her. Jane took her hand and led her in among the cardboard cartons and snow shovels. She turned around and looked at me.

"Do I have to stay here?"

"She'll feel a lot better."

"Well," Jane said, "I just want you to know that I wouldn't do it for anybody else but you."

"I like you too," I said. Then I locked the door of the shed and went back into our shop. I sat down at the front table looking innocent. A few minutes later, I saw the cops leave and drive away. From the kitchen, I got our transistor radio and put it on in the shop to listen to the news bulletins. Within a couple of hours, they were saying that the girl had been reported seen in the Yorkville area and that the police were checking this.

I was pretty sure they'd be back soon. They knew she'd been in the house last night, Walter must have told them that, and they would probably have someone watching the house in case she came back. In a couple of hours when they turned up no trace of her, they would come back and try to put more pressure on everyone in the house, threaten arrests for drugs or contributing to juvenile delinquency. Luckily no-one there saw me leave with the girl, so no amount of pressure could tip them off where she was. Which suited me just fine.

At quarter to twelve I started making lunch, and made extra of everything for the girls in the shed. I took it out on tinfoil plates, feeling like part of one of Tom Sawyer's games. Jane complained of the discomfort of the shed, so I passed in a couple of folding cots so they could lie down. All this, I tried to do in such a way that it would not look suspicious from any of the upstairs windows nearby. Good old Tom Sawyer, where would I have been without him?

It was about two o'clock when Olivia got up and wandered into the front of the shop with a towel wrapped around her.

"There's nobody here but me," I said. "You might as well get dressed."

"Spare me your wit until I wake up a bit. Where's that girl you were telling me about?"

"In our back shed."

"Not really."

"The cops came looking for her next door, so I slipped her out the back and put her in the shed."

"They're going to put you in jail, do you know that? Or they're going to send the men in white coats for you. Either way, there's

Olivia's Scrapbook 45

going to be nothing left of you around here except your clothes. Unless I keep a scrapbook of your newspaper clippings." She shook her head. "It should make quite a trial. Tell me that's why you're doing it, that it's just a publicity gimmick so the store will get mentioned in the paper. That must be it."

"I'm doing it because I don't want her put in an institution."

"Well you're going to end up in one, the way you're going. I really find it all just a little bit hard to understand. Are you going to leave her in the shed forever? You could drill a hole in the wall and charge a dime to peak in. God, when the police find her, I'll be able to charge admission to see you. The man with a hole in his head." She turned away.

"Don't phone the cops again, Olivia," I said, "or I'll break your neck."

"You're developing a taste for cheap melodama," she said as she disappeared.

I could hear her in the shower and moving around in the bedroom getting dressed. Half an hour later, she was headed out the front door. She'd just raised the hem on her shortest skirt another four or five inches. I hoped whatever she had on underneath looked good.

"I have to see some people downtown," she said.

"Just don't phone the cops," I said.

She left. I watched out the window as she walked down the street, her skinny legs very white in the sun. When she disappeared round a corner, I didn't have the energy to move away from the window, and I was still standing there when Barrow Man appeared and began pushing his empty cart along the street toward me. As he passed the window, I tapped on it and motioned him in. He left his barrow by the side of the road and came in.

"The cops were here," I said, as soon as he was inside the door.

"Did you get her out?"

"Just in time. She and Jane are in the back shed."

"What's Jane doing there?"

"It was the only way I could get the girl to go in."

Barrow Man giggled.

"I got hold of a friend of mine," he said. "Who's got a place out in the country. It's just a beaten up old farmhouse but she'll probably be all right there. He says he can use a housekeeper if she wants to work."

"That sounds fine, but how are we going to get her out of here."

"I said we'd meet him at nine-thirty tonight."

"But they'll have cops all over."

"Suppose so."

"We might just sneak her past in the dark."

"What we really need is something to attract their attention, start a riot or something."

"We could burn a house down."

"Wait a minute, wait a minute."

He was thinking. I could tell by the look on his face.

"Look," he said. "I'll light a fire on my barrow and lead the cops away with that. It'll draw a crowd for sure. Then you grab the girl and take off."

"It'll ruin your barrow."

"I'll get a new one. You got any old paint and turpentine?"

"In the back shed."

I gave him the key.

"Watch for the girl," I said. "Don't let her out."

It was at that moment that a customer came into the shop. I knew it must be a mistake and went to clear it up, but I ended up by selling something. I thought it must be some kind of omen. When I looked out the back, I saw that Barrow Man had his little cart covered with cardboard boxes that held half the old paint from the shed. If he wasn't careful he'd burn down the whole neighbourhood. He stuck his head in the back door.

"Nine-thirty tonight, okay?"

I said it was okay.

"You meet my friend two blocks up Avenue Road. A brown station wagon."

I nodded and he closed the door. I went back to work in the shop. For hours I sat and waited.

Finally, at suppertime, I brought Jane and the girl into the house. I couldn't see myself taking another meal out to the shed, and I figured they might as well be inside. After supper I turned on the television set for them, and the three of us watched it until it started to get dark. A little bit after nine, we all went into the shop and sat by the front window waiting for Barrow Man to light his fire.

At nine-fifteen he did it. It was a dandy. He must have had about ten gallons of paint and solvents on his barrow, and when they went up, one whole area of the street was lit. We could see him grab the handles of his barrow and start down a sidestreet with it.

"He's going to burn himself," Jane said.

"Or get arrested for arson," I said. "Let's go."

We led the girl out the front door and along the street away from the fire. All evening she had been looking more and more withdrawn, and now she seemed completely out of touch. We led her along dark streets and she followed, but apparently with no idea of where she was going or why. I wanted badly to talk to her, just two or three words. Anything. Jane had tried to explain to her during the day what was going on, had even printed notes for her, but we didn't know if she could read, and nothing seemed to reach her.

We approached Avenue Road a block below the meeting place we had arranged. The traffic was very heavy, and as we stood on the corner, I saw something beside me move. It was the girl who suddenly ran into the road, miraculously made her way past half a dozen speeding cars and ran down the street on the other side. Jane and I stood and watched her, helpless until the traffic slowed a bit.

By the time we got across the road, she had disappeared. For perhaps half an hour, we walked along the streets, down alleys and lanes, but there was no sign of her. We went to tell the driver that she wasn't coming, but he had gone. He must have got tired of waiting. There was nothing more we could do. We walked down Avenue Road toward home.

"Well," I said, "That's it."

"She must have been pretty frightened."

"Poor little idiot. The police will find her eventually and put her in a box."

"Maybe that's best."

"No," I said. "That's not ever best for anybody."

Jane reached out and took my hand.

"I suppose we were crazy to even try it," I said.

"Maybe."

"Tell Barrow Man I'll give him some money for a new cart."

"If I'm talking to him, I'll tell him."

We walked on down the dark streets. Jane was still holding my hand. She has big hands and feet. We didn't look at each other until we got home. Down the street where Barrow Man had lit his fire, there were still a few people hanging around.

"I wonder if the cops got Barrow Man," I said.

"I doubt it," she said.

I knew that now I had to look at her as we stood there in the street. Looked, knowing what I would see. She wanted to come in with me. And why not? Olivia wouldn't be home until morning, and if she was, she wasn't likely to say a hell of a lot, not in the circumstances. I looked down at Jane's face again. It was a wide face, not pretty, but warm and gentle. I wondered where Olivia was and what she was doing. Or having done to her. I kissed Jane on the forehead and turned away.

"I'll see you tomorrow," I said.

I walked into the house. And don't start asking me why.

Olivia's Scrapbook

John Metcalf

John Metcalf (1938-), British born, came to Canada in 1962. In Quebec he has been a high school teacher and is now a lecturer in English at Loyola College. His stories have been accepted by the CBC, and several Canadian periodicals. "The Happiest Days" is from his series "The Geography of Time." He is also the author of a collection of short stories entitled *The Lady Who Sold Furniture*.

It is rare to read a successful short short story. Many writers can render an effective anecdote through simple plot luck, but few can instil within a trifle of life the suggestiveness of a much larger context. Call it *multum in parvo*, the macrocosm within a microcosm, it is to achieve in prose what William Blake did in poetry; "To see the world in a grain of sand, And a heaven in a wild flower; Hold infinity in the palm of your hand, and eternity in an hour." The writer risks everything on a limited number of words, confident that his stripped, clean-cut prose will verify his contention that "less is more". In this assertion Metcalf is following in the tradition of Chekhov "one should be brief, as brief as possible", Katherine Mansfield, "One has to leave out what one knows and longs to use", and Somerset Maugham, "A good rule for writers: do not explain overmuch".

Point of view in "The Happiest Days" fluctuates between the first person narrator and the impersonal central intelligence. The opening two sentences exemplify this unusual shift of viewpoint from the cold objectivity of statement to the personal subjectivity of statement. Slowly the reader zeroes in directly to the schoolteacher's mind assessing his character via the clipped, monosyllabic, taut sentences. Thought is the language of silence, and through it the submerged gap between teacher and students alternately thickens and thins. The first person device gains an immediate intimacy plus the air of authenticity. The teacher's flashbacks into the past good life account for his nostalgia and present distaste for the banal conversation in the staff-room. Like Eliot's Prufrock and James Hilton's Mr. Chips, the nameless "mister" and "sir" is an introvert surrounded by extroverts, a sensitive retreater, "I flinched away as I always did." Thwarted and frustrated by his impersonal functions he vents his pent-up irritations on Fielding with disastrous results, for "still I stand there for there is no defence."

The reader is left to complete the total picture. To quote Chekhov again, "it is better to say not enough than to say too much, because — because — I don't know why! . . . I think that when one has finished writing a short story one should delete the beginning and the end." What motivation led to the teacher's outburst: envy? jealousy? cowardice? Mystery is perpendicular to language and has to be sought after between the lines. Does the repetition of the last paragraph imply any insecurity in the teacher's mind? Is he a much older boy carving marks on the "rude desks with the unfulfilled hopes"? Much can be gained by comparing the teacher with Prufrock in Eliot's famous poem. Both men endure only by measuring out their lives with coffee spoons, suffering either in passive intolerance or in ineffectual retaliation. The monotony of life is emphasized by the monosyllabic vocabulary which only occasionally relaxes from its flat uniformity. Find further parallels between the two men.

Kipling once wrote that "a tale from which pieces have been raked out is like a fire that has been poked. One does not know that the operation has been performed, but everyone feels the effect." Discuss the advantages and also the disadvantages of omission of facts in this and other stories.

The Happiest Days

The report cards are yellow with brown printing. I am filling in the numbers black Pass red Fail; the aggregate and average attendance for the months of September, October, November, and December excluding Public Holidays; Character Traits; Citizenship, Honesty, Co-operation, Practicality and Idealism.

I am secretly looking at the children. They are supposed to be working and are not. Sometimes it is like a trance. The chalk stops in the middle of its loops and squeaks, and I want to say something, but cannot. They would not understand. I want to say, "I know. I understand." I would like to rend the neat divisions of their minds, break the rules, shout "Bum."

Like an unwanted child, seeming unconcerned on the borders of the game, I watch them when they play. Twenty years young I ran with you, played the ball, knocked out imaginary teeth, and, as it seems, was happy.

Standing now in the falling chalk-dust, I say, "This is a lyric poem which rhymes *ab ab*."

In the wood was an old holly tree whose bark was scabbed and peeled like ivory. Some twenty feet above the ground a large branch formed a natural seat, and the glossy leaves made a cage around it, hiding you from view. We went there often to talk and smoke, or just to sit. I can see it clearly.

Below the large branch was a thinner one and David always used to Tarzan-drop through the terrifying space to grasp it, swinging until the bouncing stopped. He never actually said anything to me but I knew. Why should I remember that now?

Years later, I had been working some two or three years, I went back to the old town, to the wood, to the tree, and everything was still the same. The same tree, the same branches, the same boys though they were different.

We talked and I did the jump — an easy grasp — a drop of two feet, and I swung there for a moment and dropped to the ground. One of the boys said, "We do that, mister." And I said, "I know," and went away.

The children are supposed to be working, and are not. They

are supposed to be reading a book called, *Travels in the Realm of Gold.*

Today is Wednesday and it is my day for duty in the yard. The packs of boys will shout and run, flowing round me like the movements of the tide. Small boys in their first year, mustached with sherbet, play with bald tennis balls, or lick transfers onto their forearms. It is the time of year now for marbles in the cotton drawstring bags. I had a Queenie, beautiful with whorls of misty red and pale smoke-blue. Older boys, who carve the rude desks with their unfulfilled hopes, will be huddled over magazines in secret corners. I wonder if the poses are still the same. Have Naturists changed? Or do they still play ping-pong in the nude?

The cactus plants, in their sand-filled box on the window ledge, are doing very well. Once a month I water them, judiciously, with a little watering-can. The atmosphere seems to suit them, for once the green flesh bore tiny pink buds.

Soon it will be coffee time. I will line up, as I always do, and fill my cup from the urn and sit listening to people talking to me. They talk about cars and gardens. A nightmare babble of voices, early flowering miles per hour, a slight adjustment paved with granite. At night I fancy them moving into gear and revving into oblivion, where, in the mulching darkness, they battle with aphids, lost in an orgy of yams and parsnips.

Outside this room the sun is shining, white clouds. Last Sports Day it was warm too and we could supervise their games without getting a chill or having to sit on damp grass. I was in charge of high-jump, sitting by the deep orange sand behind the poles. I could see each white-clad body rise, lie black against the sky and roll gracefully into the sand. One of the boys brought me a cup of tea. It was a pleasant day. It was like a field dotted with white flowers.

Later, I was talking with some of the older boys about T. S. Eliot. *The Love Song of J. Alfred Prufrock.* I remember distinctly. We strolled about slowly in the sunlight and I talked and they listened and asked questions. It was like ancient Greece. That's a conceit, I suppose — but the javelin and discus, and the running, and the teacher with his groups of students. In a way, one of the most pleasing things of the year.

But then a mob of boys, throwing a football, ran round us and kicked the ball across our path, and, though no one seemed to notice, I flinched away as I always did.

The report cards are yellow with brown printing. Carter. Carter, John. Age, as of July 10th, fifteen years and one month. Brings bits of motorcycles to school with him and puts them on his desk, touching them lightly with his fingertips, stroking the dull metal. Language 30. Literature 32.

Dawson. Dawson, Peter. Who lives reserved and passionately for his fishing. Regardless of title, every composition is the same. "A Journey." We went a journey on the bus to the river where we started fishing. "The Day the Circus Came to Town." On the day the circus came to town I happened to be fishing. Comments. Should not waste time outside school?

Fielding. Fielding, Tony. Age, as of July, sixteen. Literature 20. Language 32. He is not reading now, though I have spoken to him twice. He is holding *Travels in the Realm of Gold* slackly in his hands and is daydreaming. In his large frame the banked fires are burning as he daydreams of the pubs he will soon enter and the tart that lives down his way you can touch in the pictures. Of the shoe factory where his dad works and where he works on Friday night and Saturday where the old women laugh and touch you. Of the fight last Thursday down the park where Geof. Brooks hit the parkie, and the half-past-eleven night shot with the gold of the chip shop and shouting at those tarts on the way home and his mother saying, "Where do you think you've been until this time!" And his father laughing and saying. "He's been chasing a bit of the other down the park," and giving him a cigarette. Yes, I can imagine it all. Literature 20. Language 32. Every single detail.

The noise has risen to a ridiculous level and I must keep them quiet. Soon Mr. Benson in the next room will hammer on the wall and they will talk about me in the staff room again. The noise of their chatter is irritating and disturbs my work.

"Silence!" I slap my hand on the desk so that it stings. They are quiet, wary, watching me to see what I will do. "You are making far too much noise. Just settle yourselves down." Tony Fielding says something to George.

"Are you deaf, Fielding?"

"No, sir."

"What was the last thing I said?"

The Happiest Days 55

"I don't know, sir."
"Why not, Fielding?"
"I expect because I wasn't listening, sir."
"Are you trying to be funny, Fielding?"
"No, sir."
"I think you're trying to be funny, Fielding. Perhaps you're not feeling well, Fielding. Perhaps you feel unwell?"
"No, sir."

I go down the row and stand over him. He is red with embarrassment. "It might be better Fielding," I say, poking his chest with my finger, "if you didn't come to school when you feel unwell. You shouldn't stay out till all hours should you, Fielding?" I cuff him on the side of the head. "You're a growing boy, Fielding. A growing boy." I prod him sharply in the chest. "It's a good job you haven't much up here," rapping the top of his head with my knuckle, "because if you had such behaviour would make your work suffer." Fielding is growing angry and confused. I take hold of his tie near the knot. "You'd be better off, Fielding, if you spent less time with that creature who hangs around the school gate for you. Wouldn't you?" I pull sharply on his tie.

He knocks away my hand and glares at me. "Would you, Fielding? You haven't got the guts." I turn away and hear him get up. At last. He pulls me round and his first punch hits me high on the shoulder. I make no defence. He hits me again, this time in the mouth and I feel the numb impact of his knuckles and then the releasing pain. He hits me again and again in the face and stomach and still I stand there for there is no defence.

The noise of their chatter is irritating and disturbs my work. The noise has risen to a ridiculous level and I must keep them quiet. Soon Mr. Benson in the next room will hammer on the wall and they will talk about me in the staff room again.

Mordecai Richler

Mordecai Richler (1931-) born in Montreal, decided to become a writer at the age of 15. Since then he has written six novels, the best known being *The Apprenticeship of Duddy Kravitz* (1959), the film scripts for *Room at the Top* and *Life at the Top*, as well as countless articles for English, Canadian and American periodicals. He now lives mainly in London: "When I return to Canada from time to time, what I always find most tiresome is the cultural protectionism, the anti-Americanism. No heritage is worth preserving unless it can survive the sun, the mixed marriage, or the foreign periodical. Culture cannot be legislated or budgeted or protected with tariffs. Like potatoes." From his earliest writings Richler has been well aware of two forms of provincialism, the Jewish and the Canadian. "To be a Jew and a Canadian," he says, "is to emerge from the ghetto twice, for self-conscious Canadians, like some touchy Jews, tend to contemplate the world through a wrong-ended telescope." Richler's talent is to have observed, collected and remembered all the essential day-to-day data of his Montreal days with two perspectives, one sympathetic the other ironic.

"Some Grist for Mervyn's Mill" is told from the "innocent eye" point of view of a young boy who, while idolizing Mervyn, is still too young to fully comprehend all the implications of the story he recounts. Because the reader can see these implications, irony is achieved as well as humour. Mervyn, the "wordsmith" takes an apprenticeship in writing and life, though the two are not always complementary. His motto, "For a writer, everything is grist to the mill. Nothing is humiliating", is similar to the advice given by the American novelist Henry James: "Try to be one of the people on whom nothing is lost." From the story's beginning

Mervyn's "electricity" is operating fully; by the end, after several short circuits, his current is waning. He generates an unprecedented concern for writing in the minds of the narrator's parents, each of whom treats Mervyn more as a son than a lodger, though it is not until the father reads one of his stories in *Liberty* that he is won over to the fledgling writer, the confident grub-streeter. The unjustified expectations of all of St. Urbain Street lead to Mervyn's crisis, his decision and his departure.

Richler's ability to construct page after page of dialogue, realistic, humourous, but above all honest and authentic, is one of the reasons for the story's success. Another is the skilful blend of compassion and irony. Mervyn's failure to get his novel published is only realized by the parents and the narrator on the last page. How early does Richler suggest to the alert reader that Mervyn is in trouble? In 1957 Richler told an interviewer that the serious writer "is not writing for money, he is writing from compulsion, I guess." Discuss how Mervyn's fate is engineered by a greedy misunderstanding of motivation. Show how through Richler's ear for the subtle nuances of dialogue we understand the psychological motivations behind Molly, her father, the narrator's parents. Will Mervyn continue to write? Richler has stated elsewhere that "Writing is an act of faith. . . . Writing is a recognition of your own mortality. And a way of cheating it." What insights into the apprenticeship and art of writing have you learned from this story?

Some Grist For Mervyn's Mill

Mervyn Kaplansky stepped out of the rain on a dreary Saturday afternoon in August to inquire about our back bedroom.

'It's $12 a week', my father said, 'payable in advance.'

Mervyn set $48 down on the table. Astonished, my father retreated a step. 'What's the rush-rush? Look around first. Maybe you won't like it here.'

'You believe in electricity?'

There were no lights on in the house. 'We're not the kind to skimp,' my father said. 'But we're orthodox here. Today is *shabus*.'

'No, no, no. Between people.'

'What are you? A wise guy?'

'I do. And as soon as I came in here I felt the right vibrations. Hi, kid.' Mervyn grinned breezily at me, but the hand he mussed my hair with was shaking. 'I'm going to love it here.'

My father watched, disconcerted but too intimidated to protest, as Mervyn sat down on the bed, bouncing a little to try the mattress. 'Go get your mother right away,' he said to me.

Fortunately, she had just entered the room. I didn't want to miss anything.

'Meet your new roomer,' Mervyn said, jumping up.

'Hold your horses.' My father hooked his thumbs in his suspenders. 'What do you do for a living?' he asked.

'I'm a writer.'

'With what firm?'

'No, no, no. For myself. I'm a creative artist.'

My father could see at once that my mother was enraptured and so, reconciled to yet another defeat, he said, 'Haven't you any . . . things?'

'When Oscar Wilde entered the United States and they asked him if he had anything to declare, he said, "Only my genius." '

My father made a sour face.

'My things are at the station,' Mervyn said, swallowing hard. 'May I bring them over?'

'Bring.'

Mervyn returned an hour or so later with his trunk, several suitcases, and an assortment of oddities that included a piece of driftwood, a wine bottle that had been made into a lamp base, a collection of pebbles, a 12-inch high replica of Rodin's 'The Thinker', a bullfight poster, a Karsh portrait of G. B. S., innumerable notebooks, a ball-point pen with a built-in flashlight, and a framed cheque for $14.85 from the *Family Herald & Weekly Star.*

'Feel free to borrow any of our books,' my mother said.

'Well, thanks. But I try not to read too much now that I'm a wordsmith myself. I'm afraid of being influenced, you see.'

Mervyn was a short, fat boy with curly black hair, warm wet eyes, and an engaging smile. I could see his underwear through the triangles of tension that ran from button to button down his shirt. The last button had probably burst off. It was gone. Mervyn, I figured, must have been at least twenty-three years old, but he looked much younger.

'Where did you say you were from?' my father asked.

'I didn't.'

Thumbs hooked in his suspenders, rocking on his heels, my father waited.

'Toronto,' Mervyn said bitterly. 'Toronto the Good. My father's a big-time insurance agent and my brothers are in ladies' wear. They're in the rat race. All of them.'

'You'll find that in this house,' my mother said, 'we are not materialists.'

Mervyn slept in — or, as he put it, stocked the unconscious — until noon every day. He typed through the afternoon and then, depleted, slept some more, and usually typed again deep into the night. He was the first writer I had ever met and I worshipped him. So did my mother. 'Have you ever noticed his hands,' she said, and I thought she was going to lecture me about his chewed-up fingernails, but what she said was, 'They're artist's hands. Your grandfather had hands like that.' If a neighbour dropped in for tea my mother would whisper, 'We'll have to speak quietly,' and, indicating the tap-tap of the typewriter from the back bedroom, she'd add, 'In there, Mervyn is creating.' My mother prepared special dishes for Mervyn. Soup, she felt, was especially nourishing. Fish was the best brain food. She discouraged chocolates and nuts because of Mervyn's complexion, but she brought him coffee at all hours, and if a day passed with no sound coming from the back room my mother would be extremely upset. Eventually, she'd knock softly on Mervyn's door. 'Anything I can get you?' she'd ask.

'It's no use. It just isn't coming today. I go through periods like that, you know.'

Mervyn was writing a novel, his first, and it was about the struggles of our people in a hostile society. The novel's title was, to begin with, a secret between Mervyn and my mother. Occasionally, he read excerpts to her. She made only one correction. 'I wouldn't say, "whore",' she said. 'It isn't nice, is it? Say "lady of easy virtue".' The two of them began to go in for literary discussions. 'Shakespeare,' my mother would say, 'Shakespeare knew everything.' And Mervyn, nodding, would reply, 'But he stole all his plots. He was a plagiarist.' My mother told Mervyn about her father, the Rabbi, and the books he had written in Yiddish. 'At his funeral,' she told him, 'they had to have six motorcycle policemen to control the crowds.' More than once my father came home from work to find the two of them still seated at the kitchen table, and his supper wasn't ready or he had to eat a cold plate. Flushing, stammering apologies, Mervyn would flee to his room. He was, I think, the only man who was ever afraid of my father, and this my father found very heady stuff. He spoke gruffly, even profanely, in Mervyn's presence, and called him Moitle behind his back. But, when you come down to it, all my father had against Mervyn was the fact that my mother no longer baked potato *kugel*. (Starch was bad for Mervyn.) My father began to spend more of his time playing cards at Tansky's Cigar & Soda, and when Mervyn fell behind with the rent he threatened to take action.

'But you can't trouble him now,' my mother said, 'When he's in the middle of his novel. He works so hard. He's a genius maybe.'

'He's peanuts, or what's he doing here?'

I used to fetch Mervyn cigarettes and headache tablets from the drugstore round the corner. On some days when it wasn't coming the two of us used to play casino and Mervyn, at his breezy best, used to wisecrack a lot. 'What would you say,' he said, 'if I told you I aim to out-Emile Zola?' Once he let me read one of his stories, 'Was the Champ a Chump?', that had been printed in magazines in Australia and South Africa. I told him that I wanted to be a writer too. 'Kid,' he said, 'a word from the wise. Never become a wordsmith. Digging ditches would be easier.'

From the day of his arrival Mervyn had always worked hard, but what with his money running low he was now so determined

Some Grist for Mervyn's Mill 61

to get his novel done that he seldom went out any more. Not even for a stroll. My mother felt this was bad for his digestion. So she arranged a date with Molly Rosen. Molly, who lived only three doors down the street, was the best looker on St Urbain, and my mother noticed that for weeks now Mervyn always happened to be standing by the window when it was time for Molly to pass on the way home from work. 'Now you go out,' my mother said, 'and enjoy. You're still a youngster. The novel can wait for a day.'

'But what does Molly want with me?'

'She's crazy to meet you. For weeks now she's been asking questions.'

Mervyn complained that he lacked a clean shirt, he pleaded a headache, but my mother said, 'Don't be afraid, she won't eat you.' All at once Mervyn's tone changed. He tilted his head cockily. 'Don't wait up for me,' he said.

Mervyn came home early. 'What happened?' I asked.

'I got bored.'

'With *Molly*?'

'Molly's an insect. Sex is highly over-estimated, you know. It also saps an artist's creative energies.'

But when my mother came home from her Talmud Torah meeting and discovered that Mervyn had come home so early she felt that she had been personally affronted. Mrs. Rosen was summoned to tea.

'It's a Saturday night,' she said, 'she puts on her best dress, and that cheapskate where does he take her? To sit on the mountain. Do you know that she turned down three other boys, including Ready-to-Wear's *only* son, because you made such a *gedille*?'

'With dumbbells like Ready-to-Wear she can have dates any night of the week. Mervyn's a creative artist.'

'On a Saturday night to take a beautiful young thing to sit on the mountain. From these benches you can get piles.'

'Don't be disgusting.'

'She's got on her dancing shoes and you know what's for him a date? To watch the people go by. He likes to make up stories about them, he says. You mean it breaks his heart to part with a dollar.'

'To bring up your daughter to be a gold-digger. For shame.'

'All right. I wasn't going to blab, but if that's how you feel — modern men and women, he told her, experiment *before* marriage. And right there on the bench he tried dirty filthy things with her. He — "

'Don't draw me no pictures. If I know your Molly he didn't have to try so hard.'

'How dare you! She went out with him it was a favour for the marble cake recipe. The dirty piker he asked her to marry him he hasn't even got a job. She laughed in his face.'

Mervyn denied that he had tried any funny stuff with Molly — he had too much respect for womankind, he said — but after my father heard that he had come home so early he no longer teased Mervyn when he stood by the window to watch Molly pass. He even resisted making wisecracks when Molly's kid brother returned Mervyn's thick letters unopened. Once, he tried to console Mervyn. 'With a towel over her face,' he said gruffly, 'one's the same as another.'

Mervyn's cheeks reddened. He coughed. And my father turned away, disgusted.

'Make no mistake,' Mervyn said with a sudden jaunty smile. 'You're talking to a boy who's been around. We pen-pushers are notorious lechers.'

Mervyn soon fell behind with the rent again and my father began to complain.

'You can't trouble him now,' my mother said. 'He's in agony. It isn't coming today.'

'Yeah, sure. The trouble is there's something coming to me.'

'Yesterday he read me a chapter from his book. It's so beautiful you could die.' My mother told him that Shalinsky, the editor of *Jewish Thought*, had looked at the book. 'He says Mervyn is a very deep writer.'

'Shalinsky's for the birds. If Mervyn's such a big writer let him make me out a cheque for the rent. That's my kind of reading, you know.'

'Give him one week more. Something will come through for him, I'm sure.'

My father waited another week, counting off the days. 'E-Day minus three today,' he'd say. 'Anything come through for the genius?' Nothing, not one lousy dime, came through for Mervyn.

Some Grist for Mervyn's Mill

In fact he had secretly borrowed from my mother for the postage to send his novel to a publisher in New York. 'E-Day minus one today,' my father said. And then, irritated because he had yet to be asked what the E stood for, he added, '*E* for *Eviction*.'

On Friday my mother prepared an enormous potato *kugel*. But when my father came home, elated, the first thing he said was, 'Where's Mervyn?'

'Can't you wait until after supper, even?'

Mervyn stepped softly into the kitchen. 'You want me?' he asked.

My father slapped a magazine down on the table. *Liberty*. He opened it at a short story titled 'A Doll for the Deacon'. 'Mel Kane, Jr,' he said, 'isn't that your literary handle?'

'His *nom de plume*,' my mother said.

'Then the story is yours.' My father clapped Mervyn on the back. 'Why didn't you tell me you were a writer? I thought you were a . . . well, a fruitcup. You know what I mean. A long-hair.'

'Let me see that,' my mother said.

Absently, my father handed her the magazine. 'You mean to say,' he said, 'you made all that up out of your own head?'

Mervyn nodded. He grinned. But he could see that my mother was displeased.

'It's a top-notch story,' my father said. Smiling, he turned to my mother. 'All the time I thought he was a sponger. A poet. He's a writer. Can you beat that?' He laughed, delighted. 'Excuse me,' he said, and he went to wash his hands.

'Here's your story, Mervyn,' my mother said. 'I'd rather not read it.'

Mervyn lowered his head.

'But you don't understand, Maw. Mervyn has to do that sort of stuff. For the money. He's got to eat too, you know.'

My mother reflected briefly. 'A little tip, then,' she said to Mervyn. 'Better he doesn't know why . . . Well, you understand.'

'Sure I do.'

At supper my father said, 'Hey, what's your novel called, Mr Kane?'

'*The Dirty Jews*.'

'Are you crazy?'

'It's an ironic title,' my mother said.

'Wow! It sure is.'

'I want to throw the lie right back in their ugly faces,' Mervyn said.

'Yeah. Yeah, sure.' My father invited Mervyn to Tansky's to meet the boys. 'In one night there,' he said, 'you can pick up enough material for a book.'

'I don't think Mervyn is interested.'

Mervyn, I could see, looked dejected. But he didn't dare antagonize my mother. Remembering something he had once told me, I said, 'To a creative writer every experience is welcome.'

'Yes, that's true,' my mother said. 'I hadn't thought of it like that.'

So my father, Mervyn, and I set off together. My father showed *Liberty* to all of Tansky's regulars. While Mervyn lit one cigarette off another, coughed, smiled foolishly, and coughed again, my father introduced him as the up-and-coming writer.

'If he's such a big writer what's he doing on St Urbain Street?'

My father explained that Mervyn had just finished his first novel. 'When that comes out,' he said, 'this boy will be batting in the major leagues.'

The regulars looked Mervyn up and down. His suit was shiny.

'You must understand,' Mervyn said, 'that, at the best of times, it's difficult for an artist to earn a living. Society is naturally hostile to us.'

'So what's so special? I'm a plumber. Society isn't hostile to me, but I've got the same problem. Listen here, it's hard for anybody to earn a living.'

'You don't get it,' Mervyn said, retreating a step. '*I'm* in rebellion against society.'

Tansky moved away, disgusted. 'Gorki, there was a writer. This boy . . .'

Molly's father thrust himself into the group surrounding Mervyn. 'You wrote a novel,' he asked, 'it's true?'

'It's with a big publisher in New York right now,' my father said.

'You should remember,' Takifman said menacingly, 'only to write good things about the Jews.'

Shapiro winked at Mervyn. The regulars smiled, some shyly, others hopefully, believing. Mervyn looked back at them solemnly.

Some Grist for Mervyn's Mill 65

'It is my profound hope,' he said, 'that in the years to come our people will have every reason to be proud of me.'

Segal stood Mervyn to a Pepsi and a sandwich. 'Six months from now,' he said, 'I'll be saying I knew you when.'

Mervyn whirled around on his counter stool. 'I'm going to out-Emile Zola.' he said. He shook with laughter.

'Do you think there's going to be another war?' Perlman asked.

'Oh, lay off,' my father said. 'Give the man air. No wisdom outside of office hours, eh, Mervyn?'

Mervyn slapped his knees and laughed some more. Molly's father pulled him aside. 'You wrote this story,' he said, holding up *Liberty*, 'and don't lie because I'll find you out.'

'Yeah,' Mervyn said, 'I'm the Grub-streeter who knocked that one off. But it's my novel that I really care about.'

'You know who I am? I'm Molly's father. Rosen. Put it there, Mervyn. There's nothing to worry. You leave everything to me.'

My mother was still awake when we got home. Alone at the kitchen table.

'You were certainly gone a long time,' she said to Mervyn.

'Nobody forced him to stay.'

'He's too polite,' my mother said, slipping her tooled leather bookmark between the pages of *Wuthering Heights*. 'He wouldn't tell you when he was bored by such common types.'

'Hey,' my father said, remembering. 'Hey, Mervyn. Can you beat that Takifman for a character?'

Mervyn started to smile, but my mother sighed and he looked away. 'It's time I hit the hay,' he said.

'Well.' My father pulled down his suspenders. 'If anyone wants to use the library let him speak now or forever hold his peace.'

'*Please, Sam.* You only say things like that to disgust me. I know that.'

My father went into Mervyn's room. He smiled a little. Mervyn waited, puzzled. My father rubbed his forehead. He pulled his ear. 'Well, I'm not a fool. You should know that. Life does things to you, but . . .'

'It certainly does, Mr Hersh.'

'You won't end up a zero like me. So I'm glad for you. Well, good night.'

But my father did not go to bed immediately. Instead, he got out his collection of pipes, neglected all these years, and sat down at the kitchen table to clean and restore them. And, starting the next morning, he began to search out and clip items in the newspapers, human interest stories with a twist, that might be exploited by Mervyn. When he came home from work — early, he had not stopped off at Tansky's — my father did not demand his supper right off but, instead, went directly to Mervyn's room. I could hear the two men talking in low voices. Finally, my mother had to disturb them. Molly was on the phone.

'Mr Kaplansky. Mervyn. Would you like to take me out on Friday night? I'm free.'

Mervyn didn't answer.

'We could watch the people go by. Anything you say. Mervyn?'

'Did your father put you up to this?'

'What's the diff? You wanted to go out with me. Well, on Friday I'm free.'

'I'm sorry. I can't do it.'

'Don't you like me any more?'

'I sure do. And the attraction is more than merely sexual. But if we go out together it will have to be because you so desire it.'

'Mervyn, if you don't take me out on Friday he won't let me out to the dance Saturday night with Solly. Please Mervyn.'

'Sorry. But I must answer in the negative.'

Mervyn told my mother about the telephone conversation and immediately she said, 'You did right.' But, a few days later, she became tremendously concerned about Mervyn. He no longer slept in each morning. Indeed, he was the first one up in the house, to wait by the window for the postman. After he had passed, however, Mervyn did not settle down to work. He'd wander sluggishly about the house or go out for a walk. Usually, Mervyn ended up at Tansky's. My father would be waiting there.

'You know,' Sugarman said, 'many amazing things have happened to me in my life. It would make *some* book.'

The men wanted to know Mervyn's opinion of Sholem Asch, the red menace, and ungrateful children. They teased him about my father. 'To hear him tell it you're a guaranteed genius.'

'Well,' Mervyn said, winking, blowing on his fingernails and rubbing them against his jacket lapel, 'who knows?'

Some Grist for Mervyn's Mill 67

But Molly's father said, 'I read in the *Gazette* this morning where Hemingway was paid $100,000 to make a movie from *one* story. A complete book must be worth at least five short stories. Wouldn't you say?' And Mervyn, coughing, clearing his throat, didn't answer, but walked off quickly. His shirt collar, too highly starched, cut into the back of his hairless, reddening neck. When I caught up with him he told me, 'No wonder so many artists have been driven to suicide. Nobody understands us. We're not in the rat race.'

Molly came by at 7.30 on Friday night.

'Is there something I can do for you?' my mother asked.

'I'm here to see Mr Kaplansky. I believe he rents a room here.'

'Better to rent out a room than give fourteen ounces to the pound.'

'If you are referring to my father's establishment then I'm sorry he can't give credit to everybody.'

'We pay cash everywhere. Knock wood.'

'I'm sure. Now may I see Mr Kaplansky, *if you don't mind?*'

'He's still dining. But I'll inquire.'

Molly didn't wait. She pushed past my mother into the kitchen. Her eyes were a little puffy. It looked to me like she had been crying. 'Hi,' she said. Molly wore her soft black hair in an upsweep. Her mouth was painted very red.

'Siddown,' my father said. 'Make yourself homely.' Nobody laughed. 'It's a joke,' he said.

'Are you ready, Mervyn?'

Mervyn fiddled with his fork. 'I've got work to do tonight,' he said.

'I'll put up a pot of coffee for you right away.'

Smiling thinly Molly pulled back her coat, took a deep breath, and sat down. She had to perch on the edge of the chair either because of her skirt or that it hurt her to sit. 'About the novel,' she said, smiling at Mervyn, 'congrats.'

'But it hasn't even been accepted by a publisher yet.'

'It's good, isn't it?'

'Of course it's good,' my mother said.

'Then what's there to worry? Come on,' Molly said, rising. 'Let's skedaddle.'

We all went to the window to watch them go down the street together.

'Look at her how she's grabbing his arm,' my mother said. 'Isn't it disgusting?'

'You lost by a TKO,' my father said.

'*Thanks,*' my mother said, and she left the room.

My father blew on his fingers. 'Whew,' he said. We continued to watch by the window. 'I'll bet you she sharpens them on a grindstone every morning to get them so pointy, and he's such a shortie he wouldn't even have to bend over to . . .' My father sat down, lit his pipe, and opened *Liberty* at Mervyn's story. 'You know, Mervyn's not that *special* a guy. Maybe it's not as hard as it seems to write stories.'

'Digging ditches would be easier,' I said.

My father took me to Tansky's for a Coke. Drumming his fingers on the counter, he answered questions about Mervyn. 'Well, it has to do with this thing . . . the Muse. On some days, with the Muse, he works better. But on other days . . .' My father addressed the regulars with a daring touch of condescension; I had never seen him so assured before. 'Well, that depends. But he says Hollywood is very corrupt.'

Mervyn came home shortly after midnight.

'I want to give you a word of advice,' my mother said. 'That girl comes from very common people. You can do better, you know.'

My father cracked his knuckles. He didn't look at Mervyn.

'You've got your future career to think of. You must choose a mate who won't be an embarrassment in the better circles.'

'Or still better stay a bachelor,' my father said.

'Nothing more dreadful can happen to a person,' my mother said, 'than to marry somebody who doesn't share his interests.'

'Play the field a little,' my father said, drawing on his pipe.

My mother looked into my father's face and laughed. My father's voice fell to a whisper. 'You get married too young,' he said, 'and you live to regret it.'

My mother laughed again. Her eyes were wet.

'I'm not the kind to stand by idly,' Mervyn said, 'while you insult Miss Rosen's good name.'

My father, my mother, looked at Mervyn, as if surprised by his presence. Mervyn retreated, startled. '*I mean that,*' he said.

'Just who do you think you're talking to?' my mother said. She looked sharply at my father.

Some Grist for Mervyn's Mill

'Hey, there,' my father said.

'I hope,' my mother said, 'success isn't giving you a swelled head.'

'Success won't change me. I'm steadfast. But you are intruding into my personal affairs. Good night.'

My father seemed both dismayed and a little pleased that someone had spoken up to my mother.

'And just what's ailing you?' my mother asked.

'Me? Nothing.'

'If you could only see yourself. At your age. A pipe.'

'According to the *Digest* it's safer than cigarettes.'

'You know absolutely nothing about people. Mervyn would never be rude to me. It's only his artistic temperament coming out.'

My father waited until my mother had gone to bed and then he slipped into Mervyn's room. 'Hi.' He sat down on the edge of Mervyn's bed. 'Tell me to mind my own business if you want me to, but . . . well, have you had bad news from New York? The publisher?'

'*I'm still waiting to hear from New York.*'

'Sure,' my father said, jumping up. 'Sorry. Good night.' But he paused briefly at the door. 'I've gone out on a limb for you. Please don't let me down.'

Molly's father phoned the next morning. 'You had a good time, Mervyn?'

'Yeah. Yeah, sure.'

'Atta boy. That girl she's crazy about you. Like they say she's walking on air.'

Molly, they said, had told the other girls in the office at Susy's Smart-Wear that she would probably soon be leaving for, as she put it, tropical climes. Gitel Shalinsky saw her shopping for beach wear on Park Avenue — in November, this — and the rumour was that Mervyn had already accepted a Hollywood offer for his book, a guaranteed best-seller. A couple of days later a package came for Mervyn. It was his novel. There was a printed form enclosed with it. The publishers felt the book was not for them.

'Tough luck,' my father said.

'It's nothing,' Mervyn said breezily. 'Some of the best word-smiths going have had their novels turned down six-seven times before a publisher takes it. Besides, this outfit wasn't for me in the first place. It's a homosexual company. They only print the pretty-pretty prose boys.' Mervyn laughed; he slapped his knees. 'I'll send the book off to another publisher today.'

My mother made Mervyn his favourite dishes for dinner. 'You have real talent,' she said to him, 'and everything will come to you.' Afterward, Molly came by. Mervyn came home very late this time, but my mother waited up for him all the same.

'I'm invited to eat at the Rosen's on Saturday night. Isn't that nice?'

'But I ordered something special from the butcher for us here.'

'I'm sorry. I didn't know.'

'So now you know. Please yourself, Mervyn. Oh, it's all right. I changed your bed. But you could have told me, you know.'

Mervyn locked his hands together to quiet them. 'Told you what, for Christ's sake? There's nothing to tell.'

'It's all right, boyele,' my mother said. 'Accidents happen.'

Once more my father slipped into Mervyn's room. 'It's okay,' he said; 'don't worry about Saturday night. Play around. Work the kinks out. But don't put anything in writing. You might live to regret it.'

'I happen to think Molly is a remarkable girl.'

'Me too. I'm not as old as you think.'

'No, no, no. You don't understand.'

My father showed Mervyn some clippings he had saved for him. One news story told of two brothers who had discovered each other by accident after twenty-five years, another was all about a funny day at court. He also gave Mervyn an announcement for the annual YMHA *Beacon* short-story contest. 'I've got an idea for you,' he said. 'Listen, Mervyn, in the movies . . . well, when Humphrey Bogart, for instance, lights up a Chesterfield or asks for a Coke, you think he doesn't get a nice little envelope from the companies concerned? Sure he does. Well, your problem seems to be money. So why couldn't you do the same thing in books? Like if your hero has to fly somewhere, for instance, why use an unnamed airline? Couldn't he go TWA because it's the safest, the best, and maybe he picks up a cutie-pie on board? Or if your central character is . . . well, a lush, couldn't he always insist on Seagram's because it's the greatest? Get the idea? I could

Some Grist for Mervyn's Mill 71

write, say, TWA, Pepsi, Seagram's, and Adam's Hats to find out just how much a book plug is worth to them, and you . . . well, what do you think?'

'I could never do that in a book of mine, that's what I think. It would reflect on my integrity. People would begin to talk, see.'

But people had already begun to talk. Molly's kid brother told me Mervyn had made a hit at dinner. His father, he said, had told Mervyn he felt, along with the moderns, that in-laws should not live with a young couple, not always, but the climate in Montreal was a real killer for his wife, and if it so happened that he ever had a son-in-law in, let's say, California . . . well, it would be nice to visit . . . and Mervyn agreed that families should be close-knit. Not all the talk was favourable, however. The boys on the street were hostile to Mervyn. An outsider, a Torontonian, they felt, was threatening to carry off our Molly.

'There they go,' the boys would say as Molly and Mervyn walked hand in hand past the poolroom, 'Beauty and the Beast.'

'All these years they've been looking, and looking, and looking, and there he is, the missing link.'

Mervyn was openly taunted on the street. 'Hey, big writer. Lard-ass. How many periods in a bottle of ink?'

'Shakespeare, come here. How did you get to look like that, or were you paid for the accident?'

But Mervyn assured me that he wasn't troubled by the boys.

'The masses,' he said, 'have always been hostile to the artist. They've driven plenty of our number to self-slaughter, you know. But I can see through them.'

His novel was turned down again.

'It doesn't matter,' Mervyn said. 'There are better publishers.'

'But wouldn't they be experts there?' my father asked. 'I mean maybe — '

'Look at this, will you? This time they sent me a personal letter! You know who this is from? It's from one of the greatest editors in all of America.'

'Maybe so,' my father said uneasily, 'but he doesn't want your book.'

'He admires my energy and enthusiasm, doesn't he?'

Once more Mervyn mailed off his novel, but this time he did

not resume his watch by the window. Mervyn was no longer the same. I don't mean that his face had broken out worse than ever — it had, it's true, only that was probably because he was eating too many starchy foods again — but suddenly he seemed indifferent to his novel's fate. 'I gave birth,' he said, 'sent my baby out into the world, and now he's on his own.' Another factor was that Mervyn had become, as he put it, pregnant once more (he looks it too, one of Tansky's regulars told me): that is to say, he was at work on a new book. My mother interpreted this as a very good sign and she did her utmost to encourage Mervyn. Though she continued to change his sheets just about every other night, she never complained about it. Why, she even pretended this was normal procedure in our house. But Mervyn seemed perpetually irritated and he avoided the type of literary discussion that had formerly given my mother such deep pleasure. Every night now he went out with Molly and there were times when he did not return until four or five in the morning. And now, curiously enough, it was my father who waited up for Mervyn, or stole out of bed to join him in the kitchen. He would make coffee and take down his prized bottle of apricot brandy. More than once I was wakened by his laughter. My father told Mervyn stories of his father's house, his boyhood, and the hard times that came after. He told Mervyn how his mother-in-law had been bedridden in our house for seven years, and with pride implicit in his every word — a pride that would have amazed and maybe even flattered my mother — he told Mervyn how my mother had tended to the old lady better than any nurse with umpteen diplomas. 'To see her now,' I heard my father say, 'is like night to day. Before the time of the old lady's stroke she was no sourpuss. Well, that's life.' He told Mervyn about the first time he had seen my mother, and how she had written him letters with poems by Shelley, Keats, and Byron in them, when all the time he had lived only two streets away and all she had to do was pick up the phone if she wanted to talk to him. But another time I heard my father say, 'When I was a young man, you know, there were days on end when I never went to bed. I was so excited. I used to go out and walk the streets better than snooze. I thought if I slept maybe I'd miss something. Now isn't that crazy?' Mervyn muttered a reply. Usually, he seemed weary and self-absorbed.

Some Grist for Mervyn's Mill

But my father was irrepressible. Listening to him, his tender tone with Mervyn and the surprise of his laughter, I felt that I had reason to be envious. My father had never talked like that to me or my brother Harvey. But I was so astonished to discover this side of my father, it was all so unexpected, that I soon forgot my jealousy.

One night I heard Mervyn tell my father, 'Maybe the novel I sent out is no good. Maybe it's just something I had to work out of my system.'

'Are you crazy it's no good? I told everyone you were a big writer.'

'It's the apricot brandy talking,' Mervyn said breezily. 'I was only kidding you.'

But Mervyn had his problems. I heard from Molly's kid brother that Mr Rosen had told him he was ready to retire. 'Not that I want to be a burden to anybody,' he had said. Molly had begun to take all the movie magazines available at Tansky's. 'So that when I meet the stars face to face,' she had told Gitel, 'I shouldn't put my foot in it, and embarrass Merv.'

Mervyn began to pick at his food, and it was not uncommon for him to leap up from the table and rush to the bathroom, holding his hand to his mouth. I discovered for the first time that my mother had bought a rubber sheet for Mervyn's bed. If Mervyn had to pass Tansky's, he no longer stopped to shoot the breeze. Instead, he would hurry past, his head lowered. Once, Segal stopped him. 'What'sa matter,' he said, 'you too good for us now?'

Tansky's regulars began to work on my father.

'All of a sudden, your genius there, he's such a B.T.O.,' Sugarman said, 'that he has no time for us here.'

'Let's face it,' my father said. 'You're zeros. We all are. But my friend Mervyn — '

'Don't tell me, Sam. He's full of beans. Baked beans.'

My father stopped going to Tansky's altogether. He took to playing solitaire at home.

'What are you doing here?' my mother asked.

'Can't I stay home one night? It's my house too, you know.'

'I want the truth, Sam.'

'Aw, those guys. You think those cockroaches know what an artist's struggle is?' He hesitated, watching my mother closely. 'By them it must be that Mervyn isn't good enough. He's no writer.'

'You know,' my mother said, 'he owes us seven weeks' rent.'

'The first day Mervyn came here,' my father said, his eyes half-shut as he held a match to his pipe, 'he said there was a kind of electricity between us. Well, I'm not going to let him down over a few bucks.'

But something was bothering Mervyn. For that night and the next he did not go out with Molly. He went to the window to watch her pass again and then retreated to his room to do the crossword puzzles.

'Feel like a casino?' I asked.

'I love that girl,' Mervyn said. 'I adore her.'

'I thought everything was okay. I thought you were making time.'

'No, no, no. I want to marry her. I told Molly that I'd settle down and get a job if she'd have me.'

'Are you crazy? A job? With your talent?'

'That's what she said.'

'Aw, let's play casino. It'll take your mind off things.'

'She doesn't understand. Nobody does. For me to take a job is not like some ordinary guy taking a job. I'm always studying my own reactions. I want to know how a shipper feels from the inside.'

'You mean you'd take a job *as a shipper*?'

'But it's not like I'd really be a shipper. It would look like that from the outside, but I'd really be studying my co-workers all the time. I'm an artist, you know.'

'Stop worrying, Mervyn. Tomorrow there'll be a letter begging you for your book.'

But the next day nothing came. A week passed. Ten days.

'That's a very good sign,' Mervyn said. 'It means they are considering my book very carefully.'

It got so we all waited around for the postman. Mervyn was aware that my father did not go to Tansky's any more and that my mother's friends had begun to tease her. Except for his endless phone calls to Molly he hardly ever came out of his room. The phone calls were futile. Molly wouldn't speak to him.

One evening my father returned from work, his face flushed. 'Son-of-a-bitch,' he said, 'that Rosen he's a cockroach. You know what he's saying? He wouldn't have in his family a faker or a swindler. He said you were not a writer, Mervyn, but garbage.' My father started to laugh. 'But I trapped him for a liar. For you know what he said? That you were going to take a job as a shipper. Boy, did I ever tell him.'

'What did you say?' my mother asked.

'I told him good. Don't you worry. When I lose my temper, you know . . .'

'Maybe it wouldn't be such a bad idea for Mervyn to take a job. Better than go into debt he could — '

'You shouldn't have bragged about me to your friends so much,' Mervyn said to my mother. 'I didn't ask it.'

'I'm a braggart? You take that back. You owe me an apology, I think. After all, *you're* the one who said you were such a big writer.'

'My talent is unquestioned. I have stacks of letters from important people and — '

'I'm waiting for an apology. Sam?'

'I have to be fair. I've seen some of the letters, so that's true. But that's not to say Emily Post would approve of Mervyn calling you a — '

'My husband was right the first time. When he said you were a sponger, Mervyn.'

'Don't worry,' Mervyn said, turning on my father. 'You'll get your rent back no matter what. Good night.'

'I can't swear to it. I may have imagined it. But when I got up to go to the toilet late that night it seemed to me that I heard Mervyn sobbing in his room. Anyway, the next morning the postman rang the bell and Mervyn came back with a package and a letter.

'Not again,' my father said.

'No. This happens to be a letter from the most important publisher in the United States. They are going to pay me $2500 for my book in advance against royalties.'

'Hey. Lemme see that.'

'Don't you trust me?'

'Of course we do.' My mother hugged Mervyn. 'All the time I knew you had it in you.'

'This calls for a celebration,' my father said, going to get the apricot brandy.

My mother went to phone Mrs Fisher. 'Oh, Ida, I just called

to say I'll be able to bake for the bazaar after all. No, nothing new here. Oh, I almost forgot. Remember Mervyn you were saying he was nothing but a little twerp? Well, he just got a fantastic offer for his book from a publisher in New York. No, I'm only allowed to say it runs into four figures in advance. Excited? That one. I'm not even sure he'll accept.'

My father grabbed the phone to call Tansky's.

'One minute. Hold it. Couldn't we keep quiet about this and have a private sort of celebration?'

My father got through to the store. 'Hello, Sugarman? Everybody come over here. Drinks on the house. Why, of Korsakov. No, wise guy. She certainly isn't. At her age? It's Mervyn. He's considering a $5000 offer just to sign a contract for his book.'

The phone rang an instant after my father had hung up.

'Well, hello, Mrs Rosen,' my mother said. 'Well, thank you. I'll give him the message. No, no, why should I have anything against you we've been neighbours for years. No. Certainly not. It wasn't *me* you called a piker. Your Molly didn't laugh in my face.'

Unnoticed, Mervyn sat down on the sofa. He held his head in his hands.

'There's the doorbell,' my father said.

'I think I'll lie down for a minute. Excuse me.'

By the time Mervyn came out of his room again many of Tansky's regulars had arrived. 'If it had been up to me,' my father said, 'none of you would be here. But Mervyn's not the type to hold grudges.'

Molly's father elbowed his way through the group surrounding Mervyn. 'I want you to know,' he said, 'that I'm proud of you today. There's nobody I'd rather have for a son-in-law.'

'You're sort of hurrying things, aren't you?'

'What? Didn't you propose to her a hundred times she wouldn't have you? And now I'm standing here to tell you all right and you're beginning with the shaking in the pants. This I don't like.'

Everybody turned to stare. There was some good-natured laughter.

'You wrote her such letters they still bring a blush to my face — '

'But they came back unopened.'

Some Grist for Mervyn's Mill 77

Molly's father shrugged and Mervyn's face turned grey as a pencil eraser.

'But you listen here,' Rosen said. 'For Molly, if you don't mind, it isn't necessary for me to go begging.'

'Here she is,' somebody said.

The regulars moved in closer.

'Hi.' Molly smelled richly of Lily of the Valley. You could see the outlines of her bra underneath her sweater (both were in Midnight Black, from Susy's Smart-Wear). Her tartan skirt was held together by an enormous gold-plated safety pin. 'Hi, doll.' She rushed up to Mervyn and kissed him. 'Maw just told me.' Molly turned to the others, her smile radiant. 'Mr Kaplansky has asked for my hand in matrimony. We are engaged.'

'Congratulations!' Rosen clapped Mervyn on the back. 'The very best to you both.'

There were whoops of approval all around.

'When it comes to choosing a bedroom set you can't go wrong with my son-in-law Lou.'

'I hope,' Takifman said sternly, ' yours will be a kosher home.'

'Some of the biggest crooks in town only eat kosher and I don't mind saying that straight to your face, Takifman.'

'He's right, you know. And these days the most important thing with young couples is that they should be sexually compatible.'

Mervyn, surrounded by the men, looked over their heads for Molly. He spotted her trapped in another circle in the far corner of the room. Molly was eating a banana. She smiled at Mervyn; she winked.

'Don't they make a lovely couple?'

'Twenty years ago they said the same thing about me. Does that answer your question?'

Mervyn was drinking heavily. He looked sick.

'Hey,' my father said, his glass spilling over, 'tell me, Segal, what goes in hard and stiff and comes out soft and wet?'

'Oh, for Christ's sake,' I said. 'Chewing gum. It's as old as the hills.'

'You watch out,' my father said. 'You're asking for it.'

'You know,' Miller said, 'I could do with something to eat.'

My mother moved silently and tight-lipped among the guests, collecting glasses just as soon as they were put down.

'I'll tell you what,' Rosen said in a booming voice, 'let's all go over to my place for a decent feed and some schnapps.'

Our living-room emptied more quickly than it had filled.

'Where's your mother?' my father asked, puzzled.

I told him she was in the kitchen and we went to get her. 'Come on,' my father said, 'let's go to the Rosens'.'

'And who, may I ask, will clean up the mess you and your friends made here?'

'It won't run away.'

'You have no pride.'

'Oh, please. Don't start. Not today.'

'Drunkard.'

'Ray Milland, that's me. Hey, what's that coming out of the wall? A bat.'

'That poor innocent boy is being railroaded into a marriage he doesn't want and you just stand there.'

'Couldn't you enjoy yourself *just once*?'

'You didn't see his face how scared he was? I thought he'd faint.'

'Who ever got married he didn't need a little push? Why, I remember when I was a young man —'

'You go, Sam. Do me a favour. Go to Rosens'.'

My father sent me out of the room.

'I'm not,' he began, 'well I'm not always happy with you. Not day in and day out. I'm telling you straight.'

'When I needed you to speak up for me you couldn't. Today courage comes in bottles. Do me a favour, Sam. Go.'

'I wasn't going to leave you alone. I was going to stay. But if that's how you feel . . .'

My father returned to the living-room to get his jacket. I jumped up.

'Where are *you* going?' he asked.

'To the party.'

'You stay here with your mother you have no consideration.'

'God damn it.'

'You heard me.' But my father paused for a moment at the door. Thumbs hooked in his suspenders, rocking to and fro on his heels, he raised his head so high his chin jutted out incongruously. 'I wasn't always your father. I was a young man once.'

'So?'

Some Grist for Mervyn's Mill

'Did you know,' he said, one eye half-shut, 'that LIVE spelled backward is EVIL?'

I woke at three in the morning when I heard a chair crash in the living-room, somebody fall, and this was followed by a sound of sobbing. It was Mervyn. Dizzy, wretched, and bewildered, he sat on the floor with a glass in his hand. When he saw me coming he raised his glass. 'The wordsmith's bottled enemy,' he said, grinning.

'When you getting married?'

He laughed. I laughed too.

'I'm not getting married.'

'Wha'?'

'Shh.'

'But I thought you were crazy about Molly?'

'I was. I am no longer.' Mervyn rose; he tottered over to the window. 'Have you ever looked up at the stars,' he said, 'and felt how small and unimportant we are?'

It hadn't occurred to me before.

'Nothing really matters. In terms of eternity our lives are shorter than a cigarette puff. Hey,' he said. 'Hey!' He took out his pen with the built-in flashlight and wrote something in his notebook. 'For a writer,' he said, 'everything is grist to the mill. Nothing is humiliating.'

'But what about Molly?'

'She's an insect. I told you the first time. All she wanted were my kudos. My fame. . . . If you're really going to become a wordsmith, remember one thing. The world is full of ridicule while you struggle. But once you've made it the glamour girls will come crawling.'

He had begun to cry again. 'Want me to sit with you for a while?' I said.

'No. Go to bed. Leave me alone.'

The next morning, at breakfast, my parents weren't talking. My mother's eyes were red and swollen and my father was in a forbidding mood. A telegram came for Mervyn.

'It's from New York,' he said. 'They want me right away. There's an offer for my book from Hollywood and they need me.'

'You don't say?'

Mervyn thrust the telegram at my father. 'Here,' he said. 'You read it.'

'Take it easy. All I said was . . .' But my father read the telegram all the same. 'Son-of-a-bitch!' he said 'Hollywood!'

We helped Mervyn pack.

'Shall I get Molly?' my father asked.

'No. I'll only be gone for a few days. I want to surprise her.'

We all went to the window to wave. Just before he got into the taxi Mervyn looked up at us; he looked for a long while, but he didn't wave, and of course we never saw him again. A few days later a bill came for the telegram. It had been sent from our house. 'I'm not surprised,' my mother said.

My mother blamed the Rosens for Mervyn's flight, while they held us responsible for what they called their daughter's disgrace. My father put his pipes aside again and naturally he took a terrible ribbing at Tansky's. About a month later, five-dollar bills began to arrive from Toronto. They came sporadically, until Mervyn had paid up all his back rent. But he never answered any of my father's letters.

Some Grist for Mervyn's Mill 81

Malcolm Lowry

Malcolm Lowry (1909-1957) settled in Vancouver at the age of 30, with a British childhood, a Cambridge education and a novel *Ultramarine* (1933) behind him. In his late teens before entering Cambridge he had shipped as a fireman's helper on a freighter to the Far East, driven to sea by the plays of Eugene O'Neill and the novels of Joseph Conrad. With the help of the American poet and novelist Conrad Aiken whose work *Blue Voyage* (1927) Lowry idolized, and a novel *The Ship Sails On* (1927) by the Norwegian writer Nordahl Grieg, he transmuted his own adventures and non-adventures at sea into *Ultramarine*. Following its publication he lived in France, New York, Hollywood, and Cuernavaca, Mexico writing short stories, poetry and novels-in-progress.

In 1940, finally finding Paradise with his second wife, Margerie, in a small waterfront shack in Dollarton on the Burrard Inlet near Vancouver, he wrote to his parents in England: "Who knows but that I might not become a Canadian Ibsen or Dostoievsky? They certainly need one. They haven't got any writers, at all: they all become Americans if they do well." In the 14 years he lived in Dollarton Lowry wrote his finest creative work, most important of which is the novel *Under the Volcano* (1947) now recognized world-wide as one of the most significant novels of the century. Looking back a few months before his death he wrote simply: "I had a childish ambition — maybe not so childish — always to contribute something to Canadian literature, and I wrote a book called *Under the Volcano*, which has become fairly well known, but which people seem to think is written by an American."

"Strange Comfort Afforded by the Profession" (1953) is the third of seven stories that make up the collection *Hear us o Lord from Heaven Thy dwelling place* (1961). Sigbjørn Wilderness is an academic biografiend, a literary corpsechewer who exalts himself into the league of Keats, Shelley, Gogol and Poe. For him, Rome is a literary necropolis wherein as a pilgrim like Dante he walks among Dead Souls, to use the title of Gogol's best known novel. Psychologically down among the dead men we see through his mind and notebook observations a morbid fascination for biographical and literary allusions, most of which you will need a dictionary and small encyclopedia to understand. It is noteworthy that Sigbjørn's encounters involve not one living person. Dead writers are his only kindred spirits. He finds life in their places of death, in "the comforting darkness of Keat's house", to use the second word in the story's title. The first word is saved for Shelley's gravestone with its inscription from Shakespeare's *The Tempest:* "Nothing of him that doth fade But doth suffer a sea-change Into something rich and strange."

Our progress through the story jumps in accordance with Sigbjørn's literary reflexes, from around Rome to Richmond to Seattle, yet we are never out of his mind or notebook. How do the unfading contents of the latter change "into something rich and strange"? How does Sigbjørn compare himself with his kindred writers: how do you think he compares with them? Like *Under the Volcano* this story is an example of life-in-death and death-in-life; similarly both works are cyclical in structure with the ending returning the reader to the beginning. There is a paradox in the story's title which pervades the narrative as a theme until, in the last paragraph, one sentence epitomizes the underlying conflicts within Sigbjørn. Discuss this inner tension in the light of Keats' term "negative capability".

Strange Comfort Afforded By The Profession

Sigbjørn Wilderness, an American writer in Rome on a Guggenheim Fellowship, paused on the steps above the flower stall and wrote, glancing from time to time at the house before him, in a black notebook:

Il poeta inglese Giovanni Keats mente maravigliosa quanto precoce mori in questa casa il 24 Febraio 1821 nel ventiseesimo anno dell' eta sua.

Here, in a sudden access of nervousness, glancing now not only at the house, but behind him at the church of Trinità dei Monti, at the woman in the flower stall, the Romans drifting up and down the steps, or passing in the Piazza di Spagna below (for though it was several years after the war he was afraid of being taken for a spy), he drew, as well as he was able, the lyre, similar to the one on the poet's tomb, that appeared on the house between the Italian and its translation:

Then he added swiftly the words below the lyre:

The young English poet, John Keats, died in this house on the 24th of February 1821, aged 26.

This accomplished, he put the notebook and pencil back in his pocket, glanced around him again with a heavier, more penetrating look — that in fact was informed by such a malaise he saw nothing at all but which was intended to say "I have a perfect right to do this," or "If you saw me do that, very well then, I *am* some sort of detective, perhaps even some kind of a painter" — descended the remaining steps, looked around wildly once more, and entered, with a sigh of relief like a man going to bed, the comforting darkness of Keats's house.

Here, having climbed the narrow staircase, he was almost instantly confronted by a legend in a glass case which said:

Remnants of aromatic gums used by Trelawny when cremating the body of Shelley.

And these words, for his notebook with which he was already rearmed felt ratified in this place, he also copied down, though he failed to comment on the gums themselves, which largely escaped his notice, as indeed did the house itself — there had been those stairs, there was a balcony, it was dark, there were many pictures, and these glass cases, it was a bit like a library — in which he saw no books of his — these made about the sum of Sigbjørn's unrecorded perceptions. From the aromatic gums he moved to the enshrined marriage license of the same poet, and Sigbjørn transcribed this document too, writing rapidly as his eyes became more used to the dim light:

Percy Bysshe Shelley of the Parish *of* Saint Mildred, Bread Street, London, Widower, *and* Mary Wollstonecraft Godwin *of* the City of Bath, Spinster, a minor, *were married in this* Church *by* Licence *with Consent of* William Godwin her father *this* Thirtieth *Day of December in the year one thousand eight hundred and sixteen.* By me Mr. Heydon, Curate. This marriage was solemnized between us.
                     PERCY BYSSHE SHELLEY
                     MARY WOLLSTONECRAFT GODWIN
In the presence of:
                     WILLIAM GODWIN
                     M. J. GODWIN.

Beneath this Sigbjørn added mysteriously:

Nemesis. Marriage of drowned Phoenician sailor. A bit odd here at all. Sad — feel swine to look at such things.

Then he passed on quickly — not so quickly he hadn't time to wonder with a remote twinge why, if there was no reason for any of his own books to be there on the shelves above him, the presence was justified of *In Memoriam, All Quiet on the Western*

Front, Green Light, and the *Field Book of Western Birds* — to another glass case in which appeared a framed and unfinished letter, evidently from Severn, Keat's friend, which Sigbjørn copied down as before:

My dear Sir:
  Keats has changed somewhat for the worse — at least his mind has much — very much — yet the blood has ceased to come, his digestion is better and but for a cough he must be improving, that is as respects his body — but the fatal prospect of consumption hangs before his mind yet — and turns everything to despair and wretchedness — he will not hear a word about living — nay, I seem to lose his confidence by trying to give him this hope [the following lines had been crossed out by Severn but Sigbjørn ruthlessly wrote them down just the same: *for his knowledge of internal anatomy enables him to judge of any change accurately and largely adds to his torture*], he will not think his future prospect favorable — he says the continued stretch of his imagination has already killed him and were he to recover would not write another line — he will not hear of his good friends in England except for what they have done — and this is another load — but of their high hopes of him — his certain success — his experience — he will not hear a word — then the want of some kind of hope to feed his vivacious imagination —

The letter having broken off here, Sigbjørn, notebook in hand, tiptoed lingeringly to another glass case where, another letter from Severn appearing, he wrote:

  My dear Brown — He is gone — he died with the most perfect ease — he seemed to go to sleep. On the 23rd at half past four the approaches of death came on. "Severn — lift me up for I am dying — I shall die easy — don't be frightened, I thank God it has come." I lifted him upon my arms and the phlegm seemed boiling in his throat. This increased until 11 at night when he gradually sank into death so quiet I still thought he slept — But I cannot say more now. I am broken down beyond my strength. I cannot be left alone. I have not slept for nine days — the days since. On Saturday a gentleman came to cast his hand and foot. On Thursday the body was opened. The lungs were completely gone. The doctors would not —

  Much moved, Sigbjørn reread this as it now appeared in his notebook, then added beneath it:

Strange Comfort 87

On Saturday a gentleman came to cast his hand and foot — that is the most sinister line to me. Who is this gentleman?

Once outside Keats's house Wilderness did not pause nor look to left or right, not even at the American Express, until he had reached a bar which he entered, however, without stopping to copy down its name. He felt he had progressed in one movement, in one stride, from Keats's house to this bar, partly just because he had wished to avoid signing his own name in the visitor's book. Sigbjørn Wilderness! The very sound of his name was like a bell-buoy — or more euphoniously a light-ship — broken adrift, and washing in from the Atlantic on a reef. Yet how he hated to write it down (loved to see it in print?) — though like so much else with him it had little reality unless he did. Without hesitating to ask himself why, if he was so disturbed by it, he did not choose another name under which to write, such as his second name which was Henry, or his mother's, which was Sanderson-Smith, he selected the most isolated booth he could find in the bar, that was itself an underground grotto, and drank two grappas in quick succession. Over his third he began to experience some of the emotions one might have expected him to undergo in Keats's house. He felt fully the surprise which had barely affected him that some of Shelley's relics were to be found there, if a fact no more astonishing than that Shelley — whose skull moreover had narrowly escaped appropriation by Byron as a drinking goblet, and whose heart, snatched out of the flames by Trelawny, he seemed to recollect from Proust, was interred in England — should have been buried in Rome at all (where the bit of Ariel's song inscribed on his gravestone might have anyway prepared one for the rich and strange), and he was touched by the chivalry of those Italians who, during the war, it was said, had preserved, at considerable risk to themselves, the contents of that house from the Germans. Moreover he now thought he began to see the house itself more clearly, though no doubt not as it was, and he produced his notebook again with the object of adding to the notes already taken these impressions that came to him in retrospect.

"Mamertine Prison," he read . . . He'd opened it at the wrong place, at some observations made yesterday upon a visit to the historic dungeon, but being gloomily entertained by what he saw, he read on as he did so feeling the clammy confined horror of that underground cell, or other underground cell, not, he suspected, really sensed at the time, rise heavily about him.

MAMERTINE PRISON [ran the heading]
   The lower is the true prison
of Mamertine, the state prison of ancient Rome.

   The lower cell called Tullianus is probably the most ancient building in Rome. The prison was used to imprison malefactors and enemies of the State. In the lower cell is seen the well where according to tradition St. Peter miraculously made a spring to baptise the gaolers Processus and Martinianus. Victims: politicians. Pontius, King of the Sanniti. Died 290 B.C. Giurgurath (Jugurtha), Aristobulus, Vercingetorix. — The Holy Martyrs, Peter and Paul. Apostles imprisoned in the reign of Nero. — Processus, Abondius, *and many others unknown* were:

        decapitato
        suppliziato (suffocated)
        strangolato
        morto per fame.

   Vercingetorix, the King of the Gauls, was certainly strangolato 49 B.C. and Jugurtha, King of Numidia, dead by starvation 104 B.C.

The lower is the true prison — why had he underlined that? Sigbjørn wondered. He ordered another grappa and, while awaiting it, turned back to his notebook where, beneath his remarks on the Mamertine prison, and added as he now recalled in the dungeon itself, this memorandum met his eyes:

   Find Gogol's house — where wrote part of Dead Souls — 1838. Where died Vielgorsky? "They do not heed me, nor see me, nor listen to me," wrote Gogol. "What have I done to them? Why do they torture me? What do they want of poor me? What can I give them? I have nothing. My strength is gone. I cannot endure all this." Suppliziato. Strangolato. In wonderful-horrible book of Nabokov's when Gogol was dying — he says — "you could feel his spine through his stomach." Leeches dangling from nose: "Lift them up, keep them away . . ." Henrik Ibsen, Thomas Mann, ditto brother: Buddenbrooks and Pippo Spano. A — where lived? became sunburned? Perhaps happy here. Prosper Mérimée and Schiller. Suppliziato. Fitzgerald in Forum. Eliot in Colosseum?

Strange Comfort   89

And underneath this was written enigmatically:

And many others.

And beneath this:

Perhaps Maxim Gorky too. This is funny. Encounter between Volga Boatman and saintly Fisherman.

What was funny? While Sigbjørn, turning over his pages toward Keats's house again, was wondering what he had meant, beyond the fact that Gorky, like most of those other distinguished individuals, had at one time lived in Rome, if not in the Mamertine prison — though with another part of his mind he knew perfectly well — he realized that the peculiar stichometry of his observations, jotted down as if he imagined he were writing a species of poem, had caused him prematurely to finish the notebook:

On Saturday a gentleman came to cast his hand and foot — that is the most sinister line to me — who is this gentleman?

With these words his notebook concluded.

That didn't mean there was no more space, for his notebooks, he reflected avuncularly, just like his candles, tended to consume themselves at both ends; yes, as he thought, there was some writing at the beginning. Reversing this, for it was upside down, he smiled and forgot about looking for space, since he immediately recognized these notes as having been taken in America two years ago upon a visit to Richmond, Virginia, a pleasant time for him. So, amused, he composed himself to read, delighted also, in an Italian bar, to be thus transported back to the South. He had made nothing of these notes, hadn't even known they were there, and it was not always easy accurately to visualize the scenes they conjured up:

The wonderful slanting square in Richmond and the tragic silhouette of interlaced leafless trees.

On a wall: *dirty stinking Degenerate Bobs was here from Boston, North End, Mass. Warp son of a bitch.*

90   The Canadian Short Story

Sigbjørn chuckled. Now he clearly remembered the biting winter day in Richmond, the dramatic courthouse in the precipitous park, the long climb up to it, and the caustic attestation to solidarity with the North in the (white) men's wash room. Smiling he read on:

In Poe's shrine, strange preserved news clippings: CAPACITY CROWD HEARS TRIBUTE TO POE'S WORKS. *University student, who ended life, buried at Wytherville.*

Yes, yes, and this he remembered too, in Poe's house, or one of Poe's houses, the one with the great dark wing of shadow on it at sunset, where the dear old lady who kept it, who'd showed him the news clipping, had said to him in a whisper: "So you see, we think these stories of his drinking can't *all* be true." He continued:

Opposite Craig house, where Poe's Helen lived, these words, upon façade, windows, stoop of the place from which E.A.P. — if I am right — must have watched the lady with the agate lamp: Headache — A.B.C. — Neuralgia: LIC-OFF-PREM — enjoy Pepsi — Drink Royal Crown Cola — Dr. Swell's Root Beer — "Furnish room for rent": did Poe really live here? Must have, could only have spotted Psyche from the regions which are Lic-Off-Prem. — Better than no Lic at all though. Bet Poe does not still live in Lic-Off-Prem. Else might account for "Furnish room for rent"?
Mem: Consult Talking Horse Friday.
— Give me Liberty or give me death [Sigbjørn now read]. In churchyard, with Patrick Henry's grave; a notice: No smoking within ten feet of the church; then:
Outside Robert E. Lee's house:
Please pull the bell
To make it ring.
— Inside Valentine Museum, with Poe's relics —

Sigbjørn paused. Now he remembered that winter day still more clearly. Robert E. Lee's house was of course far below the courthouse, remote from Patrick Henry and the Craig house and the other Poe shrine, and it would have been a good step hence to the Valentine Museum, even had not Richmond, a city whose

Hellenic character was not confined to its architecture, but would have been recognized in its gradients by a Greek mountain goat, been grouped about streets so steep it was painful to think of Poe toiling up them. Sigbjørn's notes were in the wrong order, and it must have been morning then, and not sunset as it was in the other house with the old lady, when he went to the Valentine Museum. He saw Lee's house again, and a faint feeling of the beauty of the whole frostbound city outside came to his mind, then a picture of a Confederate white house, near a gigantic red-brick factory chimney, with far below a glimpse of an old cobbled street, and a lone figure crossing a waste, as between three centuries, from the house toward the railway tracks and this chimney, which belonged to the Bone Dry Fertilizer Company. But in the sequence of his notes "Please pull the bell, to make it ring," on Lee's house, had seemed to provide a certain musical effect of solemnity, yet ushering him instead into the Poe museum which Sigbjørn now in memory re-entered.

> Inside Valentine Museum, with Poe's relics [he read once more]
> Please
> Do not smoke
> Do not run
> Do not touch walls or exhibits
> Observation of these rules will insure your own and others' enjoyment of the museum.
> — Blue silk coat and waistcoat, gift of the Misses Boykin, that belonged to one of George Washington's dentists.

Sigbjørn closed his eyes, in his mind Shelley's crematory gums and the gift of the Misses Boykin struggling for a moment helplessly, then he returned to the words that followed. They were Poe's own, and formed part of some letters once presumably written in anguished and private desperation, but which were now to be perused at leisure by anyone whose enjoyment of them would be "insured" so long as they neither smoked nor ran nor touched the glass case in which, like the gums (on the other side of the world), they were preserved. He read:

> Excerpt from a letter by Poe — after having been dismissed from West Point — to his foster father. Feb. 21, 1831.

"It will however be the last time I ever trouble any human being — I feel I am on a sick bed from which I shall never get up."

Sigbjørn calculated with a pang that Poe must have written these words almost seven years to the day after Keats's death, then, that far from never having got up from his sick bed, he had risen from it to change, thanks to Baudelaire, the whole course of European literature, yes, and not merely to trouble, but to frighten the wits out of several generations of human beings with such choice pieces as "King Pest," "The Pit and the Pendulum," and "A Descent into the Maelstrom," not to speak of the effect produced by the compendious and prophetic *Eureka*.

My ear has been too shocking for any description — I am wearing away every day, even if my last sickness had not completed it.

Sigbjørn finished his grappa and ordered another. The sensation produced by reading these notes was really very curious. First, he was conscious of himself reading them here in this Roman bar, then of himself in the Valentine Museum in Richmond, Virginia, reading the letters through the glass case and copying fragments from these down, then of poor Poe sitting blackly somewhere writing them. Beyond this was the vision of Poe's foster father likewise reading some of these letters, for all he knew unheedingly, yet solemnly putting them away for what turned out to be posterity, these letters which, whatever they might not be, were certainly — he thought again — intended to be private. But were they indeed? Even here at this extremity Poe must have felt that he was transcribing the story that was E. A. Poe, at this very moment of what he conceived to be his greatest need, his final — however consciously engineered — disgrace, felt a certain reluctance, perhaps, to send what he wrote, as if he were thinking: Damn it, I could use some of that, it may not be so hot, but it is at least too good to waste on my foster father. Some of Keats's own published letters were not different. And yet it was almost bizarre how, among these glass cases, in these museums, to what extent one revolved about, was hemmed in by, this cinereous evidence of anguish. Where was Poe's astrolabe, Keats's tankard of claret, Shelley's "Useful Knots for the Yachtsman"? It was true that Shelley himself might not have been aware of the aromatic gums, but even that beautiful and irrelevant circumstantiality that was the gift of the Misses Boykin seemed not without its suggestion of suffering, at least for George Washington.

> Baltimore, April 12, 1833.
> I am perishing — absolutely perishing for want of aid. And yet I am not idle — nor have I committed any offence against society which would render me deserving of so hard a fate. For God's sake pity me and save me from destruction.
> E. A. POE

Oh, God, thought Sigbjørn. But Poe had held out another sixteen years. He had died in Baltimore at the age of forty. Sigbjørn himself was nine behind on that game so far, and — with luck — should win easily. Perhaps if Poe had held out a little longer — perhaps if Keats — he turned over the pages of his notebook rapidly, only to be confronted by the letter from Severn:

> My dear Sir:
> Keats has changed somewhat for the worse — at least his mind has much — very much — yet the blood has ceased to come . . . but the fatal prospect hangs . . . *for his knowledge of internal anatomy . . . largely adds to his torture.*

Suppliziato, strangolato, he thought . . . *The lower is the true prison. And many others.* Nor have I committed any offense against society. Not much you hadn't, brother. Society might pay you the highest honors, even to putting your relics in the company of the waistcoat belonging to George Washington's dentist, but in its heart it cried: — *dirty stinking Degenerate Bobs was here from Boston, North End, Mass. Warp son of a bitch!* . . . "On Saturday a gentleman came to cast his hand and foot . . ." Had anybody done that, Sigbjørn wondered, tasting his new grappa, and suddenly cognizant of his diminishing Guggenheim, compared, that was, Keats and Poe? — But compare in what sense, Keats, with what, in what sense, with Poe? What was it he wanted to compare? Not the aesthetic of the two poets, nor the breakdown of *Hyperion*, in relation to Poe's conception of the short poem, nor yet the philosophic ambition of the one, with the philosophic achievement of the other. Or could that more properly be discerned as negative capability, as opposed to negative achievement? Or did he merely wish to relate their melancholias? potations? hangovers? Their sheer guts — which commentators so obligingly forgot! — character, in a high sense of that word, the sense in which Conrad sometimes understood it, for were they not in their souls like hapless shipmasters, determined to drive their leaky commands full of valuable treasure at all costs, somehow, into port, and always against time, yet through all but interminable tempest, typhoons that so rarely abated? Or merely what seemed funereally analogous within the mutuality of their shrines? Or he could even speculate, starting with Baudelaire again, upon what the French movie director Epstein who had made *La Chute de la Maison Usher* in a way that would have delighted Poe himself, might have done with *The Eve of St. Agnes: And they are gone!* . . . "For God's sake pity me and save me from destruction!"

Ah ha, now he thought he had it: did not the preservation of such relics betoken — beyond the filing cabinet of the malicious foster father who wanted to catch one out — less an obscure revenge for the poet's nonconformity, than for his magical monopoly, his possession of words? On the one hand he could write his translunar "Ulalume," his enchanted "To a Nightingale" (which might account for the *Field Book of Western Birds*), on the other was capable of saying, simply, "I am perishing . . . For God's sake pity me . . ." You see, after all, he's just like folks . . . What's this? . . . Conversely, there might appear almost a tragic condescension in remarks such as Flaubert's often quoted "Ils sont dans le vrai" perpetuated by Kafka — Kaf — and others, and addressed to child-bearing rosy-cheeked and jolly humanity at large. Condescension, nay, inverse self-approval, something downright unnecessary. And Flaub — Why should they be dans le vrai any more than the artist was dans le vrai? All people and poets are much the same but some poets are more the same than others, as George Orwell might have said. George Or — And yet, what modern poet would be caught dead (though they'd do their best to catch him all right) with his "For Christ's sake send aid," unrepossessed, unincinerated, to be put in a glass case? It was a truism to say that poets not only were, but looked like folks these days. Far from ostensible nonconformists, as the daily papers, the very writers themselves

— more shame to them — took every opportunity triumphantly to point out, they dressed like, and as often as not were bank clerks, or, marvelous paradox, engaged in advertising. It was true. He, Sigbjørn, dressed like a bank clerk himself — how else should he have courage to go into a bank? It was questionable whether poets especially, in uttermost private, any longer allowed themselves to say things like "For God's sake pity me!" Yes, they had become more like folks even than folks. And the despair in the glass case, all private correspondence carefully destroyed, yet destined to become ten thousand times more public than ever, viewed through the great glass case of art, was now transmuted into hieroglyphics, masterly compressions, obscurities to be deciphered by experts — yes, and poets — like Sigbjørn Wilderness. Wil —

And many others. Probably there was a good idea somewhere, lurking among these arrant self-contradictions; pity could not keep him from using it, nor a certain sense of horror that he felt all over again that these mummified and naked cries of agony should lie thus exposed to human view in permanent incorruption, as if embalmed evermore in their separate eternal funeral parlors: separate, yet not separate, for was it not as if Poe's cry from Baltimore, in a mysterious manner, in the manner that the octet of a sonnet, say, is answered by its sestet, had already been answered, seven years before, by Keats's cry from Rome; so that according to the special reality of Sigbjørn's notebook at least, Poe's own death appeared like something extraformal, almost extraprofessional, an afterthought. Yet inerrably it was part of the same poem, the same story. "And yet the fatal prospect hangs . . ." "Severn, lift me up, for I am dying." "Lift them up, keep them away." Dr. Swell's Root Beer.

Good idea or not, there was no more room to implement his thoughts within this notebook (the notes on Poe and Richmond ran, through Fredericksburg, into his remarks upon Rome, the Mamertine Prison, and Keats's house, and vice versa), so Sigbjørn brought out another one from his trousers pocket.

This was a bigger notebook altogether, its paper stiffer and stronger, showing it dated from before the war, and he had brought if from America at the last minute, fearing that such might be hard to come by abroad.

In those days he had almost given up taking notes: every new notebook bought represented an impluse, soon to be overlaid, to write afresh; as a consequence he had accumulated a number of notebooks like this one at home, yet which were almost empty, which he had never taken with him on his more recent travels since the war, else a given trip would have seemed to start off with a destructive stoop, from the past, in its soul: this one had looked an exception so he'd packed it.

Just the same, he saw, it was not innocent of writing: several pages at the beginning were covered with his handwriting, so shaky and hysterical of appearance, that Sigbjørn had to put on his spectacles to read it. Seattle, he made out. July? 1939. Seattle! Sigbjørn swallowed some grappa hastily. Lo, death hath reared himself a throne in a strange city lying alone far down within the dim west, where the good and the bad and the best and the rest, have gone to their eternal worst! The lower is the true Seattle . . . Sigbjørn felt he could be excused for not fully appreciating Seattle, its mountain graces, in those days. For these were not notes he had found but the draft of a letter, written in the notebook because it was that type of letter possible for him to write only in a bar. A bar? Well, one might have called it a bar. For in those days, in Seattle, in the state of Washington, they still did not sell hard liquor in bars — as, for that matter, to this day they did not, in Richmond, in the state of Virginia — which was half the gruesome and pointless point of his having been in the state of Washington. LIC-OFF-PREM, he thought. No, no, go not to Virginia Dare . . . Neither twist Pepso — tight-rooted! — for its poisonous bane. The letter dated — no question of his recognition of it, though whether he'd made another version and posted it he had forgotten — from absolutely the lowest ebb of those low tides of his life, a time marked by the baleful circumstance that the small legacy on which he then lived had been suddenly put in charge of a Los Angeles lawyer, to whom this letter indeed was written, his family, who considered him incompetent, having refused to have anything further to do with him, as, in effect, did the lawyer, who had sent him to a religious-minded family of Buchmanite tendencies in Seattle on the understanding he be entrusted with not more than 25c a day.

Strange Comfort 97

Dear Mr. Van Bosch:

It is, psychologically, apart from anything else, of extreme urgency that I leave Seattle and come to Los Angeles to see you. I fear a complete mental collapse else. I have cooperated far beyond what I thought was the best of my ability here in the matter of liquor and I have also tried to work hard, so far, alas, without selling anything. I cannot say either that my ways have been as circumscribed exactly as I thought they would be by the Mackorkindales, who at least have seen my point of view on some matters, and if they pray for guidance on the very few occasions when they do see fit to exceed the stipulated 25c a day, they are at least sympathetic with my wishes to return. This may be because the elder Mackorkindale is literally and physically worn out following me through Seattle, or because you have failed to supply sufficient means for my board, but this is certainly as far as the sympathy goes. In short, they sympathize, but cannot honestly agree; nor will they advise you I should return. And in anything that applies to my writing — and this I find almost the hardest to bear — I am met with the opinion that I "should put all that behind me." If they merely claimed to be abetting yourself or my parents in this it would be understandable, but this judgment is presented to me independently, somewhat blasphemously in my view — though without question they believe it — as coming directly from God, who stoops daily from on high to inform the Mackorkindales, if not in so many words, that as a serious writer I am lousy. Scenting some hidden truth about this, things being what they are, I would find it discouraging enough if it stopped there, and were not beyond that the hope held out, miraculously congruent also with that of my parents and yourself, that I could instead turn myself into a successful writer of advertisements. Since I cannot but feel, I repeat, and feel respectfully, that they are sincere in their beliefs, all I can say is that in this daily rapprochement with their Almighty in Seattle I hope some prayer that has slipped in by mistake to let the dreadful man for heaven's sake return to Los Angeles may eventually be answered. For I find it impossible to describe my spiritual isolation in this place, nor the gloom into which I have sunk. I enjoyed of course the seaside — the Mackorkindales doubtless reported to you that the Group were having a small rally in Bellingham (I wish you could go to Bellingham one day) — but I have completely exhausted any therapeutic value in my stay. God knows I ought to know, I shall never recover in this place, isolated as I am from Primrose who, whatever you may say, I want with all my heart to make my wife. It was the greatest of anguish that I discovered that her letters to me were being opened, finally, even having to hear lectures on her moral character by those who had read these letters, which I had thus been prevented from replying to, causing such pain to her as I cannot think of. This separation from her would be an unendurable agony, without anything else, but as things stand I can only say I would be better off in a prison, in the worst dungeon that could be imagined, than to be incarcerated in this damnable place with the highest suicide rate in the Union. Literally I am dying in this macabre hole and I appeal to you to send me, out of the money that is after all mine, enough that I may return. Surely I am not the only writer, there have been others in history whose ways have been misconstrued and who have failed . . . who have won through . . . success . . . publicans and sinners . . . I have no intention ——

Sigbjørn broke off reading, and resisting an impulse to tear the letter out of the notebook, for that would loosen the pages, began meticulously to cross it out, line by line.

And now this was half done he began to be sorry. For now, damn it, he wouldn't be able to use it. Even when he'd written it he must have thought it a bit too good for poor old VanBosch, though one admitted that wasn't saying much. Wherever or however he could have used it. And yet, what if they had found his letter — whoever "they" were — and put it, glass-encased, in a museum among *his* relics? Not much — Still, you never knew! — Well, they wouldn't do it now. Anyhow, perhaps he would remember enough of it . . . "I am dying, absolutely perishing." "What have I done to them?" "My dear Sir." "The worst dungeon." And many others: and *dirty stinking Degenerate Bobs was here from Boston, North End, Mass. Warp son* — !

Sigbjørn finished his fifth unregenerate grappa and suddenly gave a loud laugh, a laugh which, as if it had realized itself it should become something more respectable, turned immediately into a prolonged — though on the whole relatively pleasurable — fit of coughing. . . .

FURTHER READING FOR ENJOYMENT

Blais, Marie-Claire. *Mad Shadows.* Toronto: McClelland and Stewart, 1960. *Tête Blanche.* Boston Little, Brown & Co., 1961. *A Season in the Life of Emmanuel.* Farrar, Straus & Giroux, New York, 1966.

Callaghan, Morley. *Morley Callaghan's Stories.* Toronto: Macmillan, 1959.

Clark, Greg. *May Your First Love Be Your Last.* Toronto: McClelland and Stewart, 1969.

Drainie, John. *Stories with John Drainie.* Toronto: Ryerson, 1963.

Engel, Marian. *No Clouds of Glory.* (Toronto: Longmans, 1968.)

Gallant, Mavis. *My Heart is Broken.* New York: Random House, 1964.

Garner, Hugh. *Hugh Garner's Best Stories.* Toronto: Ryerson, 1963.
Men and Women. Toronto: Ryerson, 1966.

Giguere, Diane. *Whirlpool.* Toronto: McClelland & Stewart, 1966.

Godfrey, Dave. *Death Goes Better With Coca-Cola.* Toronto: House of Anansi, 1967.

Helwig, David. *The Streets of Summer.* Ottawa: Oberon, 1969.

Hood, Hugh. *Flying a Red Kite.* Toronto: Ryerson, 1962.
White Figure, White Ground. Toronto: Ryerson, 1964.
Around the Mountain: Scenes from Montreal Life. Toronto: Peter Martin, 1967.
The Camera Always Lies. Toronto: Longmans, 1967.
Strength Down Centre: The Jean Beliveau Story. Toronto: Prentice Hall, 1970.

Klinck, Carl, F. *Literary History of Canada.* Toronto: U. of T. Press, 1965.

Knister, Raymond. ed. *Canadian Short Stories.* Toronto: Macmillan, 1928.

Kreisel, Henry. ed. *Klanak Islands.* Vancouver: Klanak Press, 1959.

Laurence, Margaret. *The Tomorrow-Tamer: Short Stories.* London: Macmillan, 1963.
A Bird in the House. Toronto: McClelland & Stewart, 1970.

Layton, Irving. *The Swinging Flesh.* Toronto: McClelland & Stewart, 1961.

Leacock, Stephen. *How to Write.* New York: Dodd, Mead & Co. 1946.
Arcadian Adventures With the Idle Rich. Toronto: McClelland & Stewart, 1958.
Sunshine Sketches of a Little Town. Toronto: McClelland & Stewart, 1960.

Levine, Norman. *Canadian Winter's Tales.* Toronto: Macmillan, 1968.

Lowry, M. *Hear Us O Lord From Heaven Thy Dwelling Place.* Philadelphia: Lippincott, 1961.
Under the Volcano. Toronto: Signet, 1966.

Martin, Claire, *Avec ou Sans Amour (nouvelles)*. Montreal: Le Cercle du Livre de France, 1958.

Metcalf, John, Spettigue, D. O., Newman, C. J. *New Canadian Writing* Toronto: Clarke, Irwin & Co., 1969.

Munro, Alice. *Dance of the Happy Shades*. Toronto: Ryerson, 1968.

Nowlan, Alden. *Miracle at Indian River*. Toronto: Clarke Irwin, 1968.

Parker, Gilbert. *Pierre and his People*. New York: Scribner's, 1912.

Pilon, Jean-guy. ed. *Liberté Douze écrivains, Douze nouvelles*. Vol. 11 #2-March-April 1969.

Raddall, Thomas H. *At the Tide's Turn and Other Stories*. Toronto: McClelland & Stewart, 1959.

Richler, Mordecai. *The Street*. Toronto: McClelland & Stewart, 1969.
Son of a Smaller Hero. New York: Paperback Library, 1965.
The Incomparable Atuk. Toronto: McClelland and Stewart, 1965.
The Apprenticeship of Duddy Kravitz. London: Penguin, 1964.
Cocksure. Toronto: McClelland and Stewart, 1968.

Rimanelli, Giose & Ruberto. ed. *Modern Canadian Stories*. Toronto: Ryerson, 1966.

Ross, Sinclair. *The Lamp at Noon and other Stories*. Toronto: McClelland & Stewart, 1968.

Seton, Ernest Thompson. *Wild Animals I Have Known*. New York: Bantam, 1946.

Smith, A. J. M. *The Book of Canadian Prose Vol. II*. Canadian Literature in English 1867–1967, Toronto: Gage, 1970.

St. Pierre, Paul. *The Chilcotin Holiday*. Toronto: McClelland & Stewart 1970.

Stein, David Lewis; Blaise, Clark; Godfrey, Dave. *New Canadian Writing*. Toronto: Clarke, Irwin & Co., 1968.

Sylvestre, G.; Conron, B.; Klinck, C. F. *Canadian Writers*. Toronto: Ryerson, 1966.

Taylor, J. Chesley ed. *The Short Story: Fiction in Transition*. New York: Scribner's, 1969.

Thériault, Adrien. (Thério) ed. *Conteurs Canadiens Français: époque contemporaine*. anthology of short stories. Montreal: Librairie Deom, 1936-1965. (1965)

Thomas, Audrey Callahan. *Ten Green Bottles*. New York: Bobbs-Merrill, 1967.

Wainwright, Andy. ed. *Notes for a Native Land*. Ottawa: Oberon, 1969.

Warwick, Jack. *The Long Journey: Literary Themes of French Canada*. Toronto: U of T. Press, 1968.

Weaver, Robert. ed. *Ten for Wednesday Night*. Toronto: McClelland & Stewart, 1961.
    ed. *Canadian Short Stories*. London: Oxford, 1962.
    ed. *Canadian Short Stories Second Series*. London: Oxford, 1968.
Wilson, Ethel. *Mrs. Golightly & Other Stories*. Toronto: Macmillan, 1961.

SOURCES FOR REFERENCE

Cook, Dorothy and Monro, Isabel. *Short Story Index*. New York, Wilson, 1953.

Green, H. G. and Sylvestre, G. *A Century of Canadian Literature*. Toronto, Ryerson, 1965.

Hamilton, Robert. *Canadian Quotations and Phrases*. Toronto. McClelland & Stewart.

Kenyon Review. *The International Symposium on the Short Story*. Part 1 #121, Oct. 68; Part 2 #123, Jan. 69; Part 3 #126, Oct. 1969.

Klinck, Carl ed. *Literary History of Canada*. Toronto, University of Toronto, 1965.

O'Connor, Frank. *The Lonely Voice, A Study of the Short Story*. Cleveland World, 1963.

Pacey, Desmond. *Creative Writing in Canada*. Toronto, Ryerson, 1961. *A Book of Canadian Stories*. Toronto, Ryerson, 1967.

Story, Norah. *The Oxford Companion to Canadian History and Literature*. Toronto, Oxford, 1967.

Tougas, G. *History of French Canadian Literature*. Toronto, Ryerson, 1966. ed. *Littérature Canadienne-Française Contemporaine*. Toronto, Oxford, 1969.

Watters, Reginald. *A Check List of Canadian Literature and Background Materials. 1628-1950*. Toronto, University of Toronto Press, 1959.

Watters and Bell, Inglis. *On Canadian Literature 1806-1960*. Toronto, University of Toronto ,1966.